5̲ ²⁰⁰¹

ω

At The Rate She Was Going, She'd Be The Town's Resident Old Maid By Forty!

Rebecca could just see her personal ad in *Valley Singles: Middle-aged virgin desperately seeks any more-or-less desirable man.*

She aimed a covert glance at her new employer, Dr. John Saville. He looked a bit bedraggled this morning. Or, as she used to mispronounce the word, *bed*-raggled. His normally neat hair was slightly tousled, and there was a heaviness to his eyelids, a rather sexy heaviness that drew Rebecca in at first glance.

That was surely how he would look in the morning after a long night of lovemaking. That was how his lover would see him when she first opened her eyes, the tousled dark hair, the sleep-heavy gaze, and then his mouth that would…

She startled herself out of her reverie. Going down that road was insane, and she would not do it. Never. *Absolutely never.* But how was she going to fix her "virginity problem" when the only man who excited her was the man she'd sworn off…?

Dear Reader,

Welcome to the world of Silhouette Desire, where you can indulge yourself every month with romances that can only be described as passionate, powerful and provocative!

The incomparable Diana Palmer heads the Desire lineup for March. *The Winter Soldier* is a continuation of the author's popular cross-line miniseries, SOLDIERS OF FORTUNE. We're sure you'll enjoy this tale of a jaded hero who offers protection in the form of a marriage of convenience to a beautiful woman in jeopardy.

Bestselling author Leanne Banks offers you March's MAN OF THE MONTH, a tempting *Millionaire Husband*, book two of her seductive miniseries MILLION DOLLAR MEN. The exciting Desire continuity series TEXAS CATTLEMAN'S CLUB: LONE STAR JEWELS continues with *Lone Star Knight* by Cindy Gerard, in which a lady of royal lineage finds love with a rugged Texas cattle baron.

The M.D. Courts His Nurse as Meagan McKinney's miniseries MATCHED IN MONTANA returns to Desire. And a single-dad rancher falls for the sexy horsetrainer he unexpectly hires in Kathie DeNosky's *The Rough and Ready Rancher*. To cap off the month, Shawna Delacorte writes a torrid tale of being *Stormbound with a Tycoon*.

So make some special time for yourself this month, and read all six of these tantalizing Silhouette Desires!

Enjoy!

Joan Marlow Golan

Joan Marlow Golan
Senior Editor, Silhouette Desire

Please address questions and book requests to:
Silhouette Reader Service
U.S.: 3010 Walden Ave., P.O. Box 1325, Buffalo, NY 14269
Canadian: P.O. Box 609, Fort Erie, Ont. L2A 5X3

The M.D. Courts His Nurse

MEAGAN McKINNEY

Published by Silhouette Books
America's Publisher of Contemporary Romance

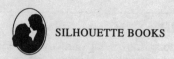

SILHOUETTE BOOKS

ISBN 0-373-76354-9

THE M.D. COURTS HIS NURSE

Visit Silhouette at www.eHarlequin.com

Printed in U.S.A.

Books by Meagan McKinney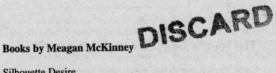

Silhouette Desire

One Small Secret #1222
*The Cowboy Meets His Match #1299
*The M.D. Courts His Nurse #1354

Silhouette Intimate Moments

*The Lawman Meets His Bride #1037

*Matched in Montana

MEAGAN McKINNEY

is the author of over a dozen novels of hardcover and paperback historical and contemporary women's fiction. In addition to romance, she likes to inject mystery and thriller elements into her work. Currently she lives in the Garden District of New Orleans with her two young sons, two very self-entitled cats and a crazy red mutt. Her favorite hobbies are traveling to the Arctic and, of course, reading!

This book is dedicated to Judd and Jude.

I couldn't have done it without you guys.

One

"I just figured out why men get smarter during sex," Lois Brubaker announced in a sly undertone, even though the waiting room was presently empty.

Rebecca O'Reilly, busy updating patient files at her wide glass-and-chrome desk, glanced up at her friend and co-worker. For a few confused moments she almost replied seriously, "They do?" Then she realized it was a joke, and she flushed slightly at the unintended reminder of her own sexual ignorance.

But she obligingly fished for the punchline. "Why?"

"Because they're plugged in to a genius," Lois replied in a deadpan manner.

A heartbeat later both women burst into laughter just as the door to the examination room swung open. Dr. John Saville emerged, escorting an elderly, moon-faced woman who wore a pullover tunic with a broomstick-pleated skirt.

Rebecca's laughter died on her lips when John Saville's

eyes, an intensely deep cobalt-blue, seemed to lash at her like whips. He frowned, a deep crease appearing between his eyebrows.

But he stoically ignored her and Lois, walking his elderly patient into the waiting room with its leather-and-chrome furniture and fresh lilacs in wicker baskets. Old-time lithographs of Mystery Valley roundup scenes decorated each pastel painted wall. The decor said homey but high priced, and John Saville's rates only made the talented young surgeon that much more exclusive and valuable in the eyes of his patients.

"You needn't worry about your nightly glass of wine, Esther," he assured her. "Especially since you have it with dinner."

"Glass—or two?" She seemed prepared to bargain.

That coaxed a smile out of him. "Yes, even two glasses, so long as you don't mean one-quart glasses."

Esther Miller laughed and placed a flirtatious hand on his arm. "I was afraid you might not approve," she confessed. "You seem so *stern,* Dr. Saville. Old Dr. Winthrop was a regular talk-show host—you know, always kidding around. A caution to screech owls, as my uncle Stan used to say. Not that I'm complaining, mind you. You seem like a *very* capable young man. And handsome—my lands! I admit I scheduled my operation early just to meet you and see what all the fuss was about. Next time I may even forego the anesthetic just to watch you in action."

For a moment Rebecca gloated when John Saville, obviously nonplussed by such candor, actually flushed until his smooth-shaven cheeks looked sunburned.

He's stern, all right, she thought. In fact, the man who prescribes your medicine, Esther, is one bitter pill himself—though it certainly did come in an attractive package.

"I'll see you at your next appointment, Esther," he replied so stiffly that Lois and Rebecca exchanged a secret smirk. The pill never did know how to take a compliment. It would require way too much loosening up, and that was something Dr. Dry-As-Dust never did.

But even Rebecca conceded that her new employer was handsome—dangerously so. He was the wrong kind of handsome for his chosen profession. His aristocratic face, athletic build, golden tan and intense eyes conveyed the impression of a French tennis star or a soap opera heart-throb, not a dedicated and brilliant surgeon who ran a thriving private practice, was on twenty-four-hour call at Valley General in nearby Lambertville and still managed to present his published research at several medical conventions each year.

But his good looks were a total, tragic waste, at least where she was concerned. While he was warm and concerned with his patients, with his employees Jekyll became Hyde and started throwing attitude around.

Just like Brian had done to her.

A thick lump of unwanted emotion clogged her throat. She'd told herself for months that Brian was the past, and someone better was the future. But it still didn't make the hurt go away. Brian had been her love, her light, her hope for more than two years. She'd met him at the beginning of his physician's internship at Lutheran Hospital—a man who wanted to heal with her by his side. They'd talked of the future, of children and of building a practice together.

By the end, however, Dr. Brian Gage could only talk about what class of Mercedes he wanted to upgrade to, and what golf community he was going to build his mansion in when he got his chance to wave goodbye to hicksville Mystery, Montana.

He upgraded his fiancée too, exchanging good old small-town Becky for a much better class of trophy wife; one who hadn't grown up poor; one who hadn't grown up struggling. One who didn't wear nurse's scrubs and who had no more ambition to help her fellow human than Marie Antoinette.

Even now Rebecca cursed herself for the bitterness. It was still there, lurking in her heart when she thought she'd scoured it out for good. She was bound and determined that Brian wasn't going to ruin her, and he hadn't. His rejection still stung, but she'd gone on with her life. She even had some hope left for the future. Her only caveat was that her future would contain no more doctors. Not even handsome ones.

And Dr. John Saville was handsome enough to be a threat.

It was sure a good thing that he was such a pill. Otherwise, as she told herself in a fit of brutal honesty, she might find herself attracted once more to the flame that had almost killed her.

"Miss O'Reilly, may I see you in my office, please?"

She looked up. The doctor stood over her desk, those laser-blue eyes focused straight on her.

She nodded. Even now, after two weeks of working with him, his imperious, autocratic manner struck her as more appropriate to a dictator than a doctor. Especially since she'd already had plenty of experience with men who treated her like a lump of gravel on *their* launch pads.

My word, she thought, we've been working together day in and day out, and he's still "Doctor," his office nurse still "Miss O'Reilly." All the stilted formality made him seem intent on reminding others of their subordinate place in life. And, oh how she hated it.

She stood, sorely missing retired Paul Winthrop's old-world charm and easy smile. He never made her or anyone else feel as if they belonged to an inferior caste.

"Of course, Doctor," she replied, knowing full well what was coming. She watched his ramrod-straight back retreat down the hall toward his private office at the rear.

"Sorry, Becky," Lois told her, keeping her voice down. "I should've saved the joke for lunchtime."

"Oh, baloney," she assured the office manager. "We weren't doing anything wrong. Laughter is good medicine, right? I'm sick of the way he acts as if this place is a funeral home. Cover my phone for me, Lo?"

Lois nodded. She was in her late thirties with stiffly sculpted blond hair and a pleasant face. "Now remember you've got that hair-trigger Irish temper," she cautioned her younger co-worker. "He's still new, we'll have to break him in gradually."

Rebecca stood up, smoothing her skirt with both hands.

John Saville had left the door open for her. He stood poker rigid in front of his neat desk, arms folded over his chest.

For an absurd moment she felt as if she was back in high school, reporting to the principal's office. Except that Mr. McNulty wasn't a bronzed hunk and a half who wore hand-sewn silk ties and Bond Street jackets.

"Yes, Doctor?" she said from the doorway.

His stern visage seemed to rearrange itself in surprise as his gaze took in this full-frontal view of her in the soft, indirect lighting. Unlike hospital nurses, she was not required to wear a uniform, and for a few moments he studied her plum-colored V-neck dress with its wide, flowing skirt. As usual, her long, chestnut hair was combed back and held in place with barrettes. The hairstyle only highlighted her brow, now furrowed in irritation, and eyes that were once called "snapping-blue."

"You wanted to see me?" she prompted again.

"Yes, right—of course." He seemed to collect himself, and the stiff formality was back. "Please come in."

She did, but he remained standing so she did, too.

The window beside his double row of file cabinets was cracked open a few inches. It was early May, and though the nights still had a nip to them, the days were sunny and growing warmer. Outside, the box elders and dogwoods that grew throughout Mystery were budding into leaf.

"Miss O'Reilly," he began again, gathering steam now, "would it be at all possible for you and Mrs. Brubaker to practice a bit more…professional decorum on the job?"

She remembered Lois's warning—and even with her heart speeding up, she admitted she really did have a temper.

But beneath all the anger was a tightly coiled spring of hurt and rejection. It hadn't been quite six months since Brian had finished his medical internship and dropped her like a bad habit.

It took conscious self-control when she replied, "I'm not sure what you mean, Dr. Saville, by professional decorum."

"What I mean," he said tightly, "is that you both need to be more professional about your work. Is that clear enough?"

His tone instantly made her combative. But she remembered to let the first flush of anger pass before she answered. "Is there some problem with my competence as a nurse? Or Lo's as office manager?"

"Competence?" he repeated. That deep crease between his eyebrows was back as he frowned at her question.

"Yes. I mean, are there problems with medical mistakes? Or have any patients complained about my manner?"

"Well…no. It's nothing like that. Just as Dr. Winthrop assured me, you are quite efficient and knowledgeable. You and Mrs. Brubaker both. It's just…"

"Just what, Doctor?"

His glance touched her and quickly slid away. Now, as he finally remembered his specific grievance, a little irritation seeped into his tone.

"Frankly, the walls in this building are not all that thick.

Even when you lower your voices,'' he added significantly. ''And tell...off-color jokes.''

Now it was her turn to flush, although she almost laughed outright at the same time. He must have heard the ''plugged-in'' joke Lois told her.

But so what, it was harmless. The effort to control her smile alerted him that she'd caught on to his reference.

He spoke up quickly. ''It gets difficult at times to concentrate on my patients with—well, with all this loud laughter and chatter. You and Mrs. Brubaker seem to forget this is not a sorority house.''

''It's Lois, not Mrs. Brubaker,'' she retorted irritably. ''And I was a full-time working student in nursing school, so I'd know nothing about sorority life.''

As I'm sure you do, golden boy, she almost added, barely catching herself in time.

Her comment, and tone of hurt dignity, forced him into momentary silence.

She felt anger hammer at her temples. Just like all the other male doctors she knew, he was a buttoned-down, wind-up medical doll who could shatter a person's self-esteem just as effortlessly as tie up a suture. Was *he* up twenty minutes early this morning to pick those damned lilacs in the waiting room? But he acted as if such things just happened by magic, not even a polite thank-you. Humor was her only ''perk'' around here—and only a jerk would begrudge it to her.

But she cooled off a bit during his silence. ''Lois and I like to have a little harmless fun,'' she informed him with cold precision. ''The time passes faster that way.''

Obviously hearing the rough bristles in her tone, he arched his eyebrows. His mouth set itself in a grim, straight line of disapproval.

''Having fun,'' he lectured her, ''isn't the point of this

clinic. We're supposed to be health *professionals.* Frankly, I worry what the patients think about our staff."

"Dr. Saville, I realize you completed your medical studies and residency in Chicago. But this is Mystery, Montana, population four thousand. Your patients are my neighbors, folks I've grown up with all my life. They like the staff."

If a voice could frown, his did now. "I have a solid grasp of my location, Miss O'Reilly—I deliberately picked this town, I didn't just stick a pin in the map."

"I confess I can't see why it appealed to you," she told him boldly. But she didn't quite have the courage to add, *After all, we're not royalty here.*

"Look, no offense intended—"

"Well, plenty is *taken,*" she assured him, feeling the warmth of anger in her face and scalp. "You've made your point, Doctor. I've duly noted the fact that laughter and smiles irritate you. Now, unless you have more complaints I'd like to finish my inventory of the medical supplies."

For a moment there Rebecca would have sworn his ultracontrolled face showed a flicker of angry animation. If so, the chiseled-coin image was immediately back in place.

"The other complaints can wait," he assured her.

Dr. Dry-As-Dust. That's what Lois had nicknamed their stiffly choreographed boss. But all that disappeared, Rebecca reminded herself, the moment some sleek socialite in a fox jacket cape showed up. Then suddenly he became the essence of charm and joie de vivre.

She stepped out of his office, shutting the door harder than necessary, and immediately made eye contact with Lois, just then turning away from the reception window with the day's mail.

Rebecca waited until she was a few safe steps from the rear office. Then she made a fist and smote her head in jest. Close enough to Lois now that she knew Dr. Saville couldn't hear her from his office, she said in a stage whisper, "Forgive me, Doctor, for I have sinned."

Immediately Lois looked horrified, and Rebecca remembered too late how quietly his door opened. She threw a quick glance over her shoulder and saw him only five feet behind her, staring with eyes like hard blue gems. Obviously he overheard her wisecrack.

Miraculously she was reprieved by the telephone on her desk.

"I'll get it, Lo," she called too eagerly at Lois. Even as she hurried to her desk, face flaming, John Saville turned on his heel and retreated into his office again, slamming the door even more loudly than Rebecca had.

"Doctor Saville's office," she answered the phone somewhat breathlessly. "Rebecca O'Reilly speaking."

"What's going on, pecan?" a throaty voice greeted her.

"Hazel, hi."

"You sound as if you've been jogging."

"I ran to the phone," she explained. Looking at the closed door, she rolled her eyes. "And I'm sure glad you called."

"Why? Don't tell me you're actually hoping I need a doctor?"

Rebecca's voice turned serious. "You don't, do you?"

"Honey, since my surgery I'm fit as a fiddle," the notorious cattle baroness assured her. "I just called to shoot the breeze."

Rebecca felt a weight lift from her. Her mother had died from a brain tumor while Rebecca was still in junior high school. With her father's job as a freelance security consultant keeping him on the road constantly, Hazel had practically adopted her, even insisting that she stay out at the ranch when her father was gone. She still missed her mother fiercely, and the thought of anything happening to Hazel was like a cold hand wrapping her heart.

"Actually," Hazel confessed, "I'm curious as the dickens to know how your love life is getting on. Did that good-looking sales rep fellow ever ask you out? The blond who drives the Town Car?"

"No, and he'd better not. His flirting was all a smoke screen."

"No fire behind the smoke, you mean?"

"No, a *wife* behind the smoke, I mean. Last time he was here he forgot to take his wedding band off the way he usually does. Horny creep."

Hazel sighed at her end. "It's true, isn't it? The real hunks are either married, gay or cowboys."

Or snobs suffering from a bad case of "It's all about me!" Rebecca added inwardly, her glance sliding toward John Saville's closed door. Still pouting in his office, she told herself. At least she knew this conversation was safe from his sonar ears—her private line was separate from his.

"So how do you like your new boss?" Hazel probed as if plucking Rebecca's thoughts from her mind.

"I don't. For such a young man, he's sure an old sober-sides. At least with his co-workers. Or should I say, with his servant staff. It's funny. I mean, he replaced Dr. Winthrop, but *he* seems even older. And, heavens, cranky? He's always got his nose out of joint about something."

"Well, I met him briefly at the reception Dottie Bryce hosted for him. I didn't get that impression at all—his nose was perfectly in place, and so was the rest of him. He's certainly good-looking. He's well knit, as Grandma Mystery used to say of men with nice builds."

"Little appeal beyond the eighteenth hole," Rebecca insisted dismissively.

"Hmm," was all Hazel said to that—a speculative tone that Rebecca knew well by now. "Anyway," the rancher went on briskly, "I guess I would like to schedule an appointment after all."

"I thought you were fit as a fiddle?"

"Hon, even a fiddle needs its strings tuned now and then."

Hazel's ironic tone turned the words *strings tuned* into a bawdy innuendo. Rebecca couldn't help feeling it was also a little nudge from Hazel, the only person in town besides Lois who knew she was still a virgin with "untuned strings."

Hazel added quickly, "I just want to ask Dr. Saville some questions about my diet since the gall bladder surgery."

"Uh-huh," she replied skeptically as she checked Lois's appointment calendar. "Seems like a lot of female patients in the Mystery area suddenly want to discuss something with their new doctor."

"So what? We gals of a certain age aren't as finicky as you proud and stubborn little twenty-three-year-olds. That's because you don't feel Time nipping at your taut little fannies yet. *We* can feel it, in the form of gravity."

Rebecca laughed as she scheduled her friend. But Hazel was wrong about one thing—she did feel Time nipping. And the question wasn't lack of desire or fear about her first time. The one man she had felt like "giving it up to" had coldly rejected her as his social inferior. And once burned, twice shy.

"Ten o'clock next Tuesday sound all right?" she asked Hazel.

"That's hunky-dory, hon. See you then."

Even as she put the handset back in its cradle, however, Rebecca was already wondering what the sly Matriarch of Mystery was really up to.

Two

"Miss O'Reilly, when you're free, may I see you in my office?"

Only my third week under Dr. Dry-As-Dust, Rebecca thought, and I've got all his imperious tones filed like everything else in this office.

She glanced at him. The tone he used now included the hardening of his mouth, and it sure wouldn't have been so irritating if his mouth wasn't so blamed handsome.

Whatever I've done now, he's really going ballistic over it, she decided, having become a great judge of the doctor's moods after all she'd observed of him the past weeks.

But she had to admire his nearly flawless control as he stood there in the tiled hallway where the waiting room met the reception area. Only the slight twitch of the muscles of his throat hinted at his anger.

Against her will, Rebecca noticed something else: the way his shoulders were so wide they stretched his pristine oxford-cloth shirt tight across his chest. Even the simple act of removing a pen from his shirt pocket showed the lines of his muscles. Another irritation. If he was going to look so good, why couldn't the man have a corresponding personality to go with it.

She'd never know why God was so fickle.

"Miss O'Reilly?" he repeated impatiently, still watching her from a stern frown. His arrogant tone made her instantly feel hostile again.

"Yes, Doctor, of course. I'll be there as soon as I've checked in everyone in the waiting room."

No trace of their personal clashing showed in her face, for the day's patients had arrived. First on the appointment calendar was Elizabeth Kent, two years older than Rebecca, who had requested a consultation regarding minor surgery to remove bone spurs in her heel. Rebecca had noticed how, ever since John took over the practice, so many women in Mystery Valley had suddenly decided to take care of various elective surgeries they had been postponing.

And they showed up dressed to the nines, looking far more gorgeous than they had bothered to look for Dr. Winthrop. Elizabeth, for example, wore a graceful garland-print dress of crepe de chine silk. And her neatly coiffed hair suggested she had just come from the salon.

But Brennan Webb, too, had already shown up, exactly forty-five minutes early, as he always was. Brennan was eighty-one, frail but courtly, and had always been one of Dr. Winthrop's—and Rebecca's—favorite patients. He sat, content and in no hurry, in the waiting room's most uncomfortable chair, an uncushioned ladderback. He wore a ranch suit with a square-tipped bow tie, an American-flag pin in his lapel. Brennan liked to boast that he was "still strong as horse radish."

"You sure you don't want the headphones and remote, Brennan?" she offered, deliberately taking her time to anger her waiting boss. "Won't take me a second to turn the TV on for you."

He waved off her suggestion. "I get enough of that crap at home, honey," he groused at her. "I get more 'n' fifty channels, hardly any of 'em worth a tinker's damn."

Immediately, however, Brennan altered his tone and added, with no logical connection, "This new doctor is young, but I'm told he knows *B* from a bull's foot, all right."

"Yes, he's certainly a blessing," Rebecca drawled with mild irony.

Not mild enough, however, to fool Brennan.

Fancy bridgework brightened the old man's big smile. But he replied in a phony, quavering tone, "Methinks you protest too much, dearie, but I'm just a senile old man. What would I know?"

"Senile schmenile," she tossed back at him, choosing to ignore his sly hint that romance was in the air. She also ignored the dirty look Elizabeth sent her way.

Since John Saville's arrival in town, the young and available women treated her like a rival for the doctor's attention, not the office nurse.

Even old curmudgeon Brennan has been sucked in, she marveled as she headed down the hallway toward John Saville's private office. The whole town acted as though Apollo had just descended into Mystery Valley from Mount Olympus.

Lois was alone in examination room A, setting up Rebecca's station for initial patient screening before Brennan saw the doctor.

Their eyes met as they passed in the hallway.

Rebecca paused a moment. "I'll be ready in a few minutes."

Lois nodded.

Rebecca didn't have to explain where she was headed—Lois had overheard Dr. Saville's strained request.

"Temper, temper," she reminded Rebecca quietly. "That vein is pulsing in your left temple."

"I'm fine," she insisted. "You're right, we just need to play it cool and break him in right. I'm *not* going to lose it around him."

Lois, however, had worked with Rebecca going on six years now and trusted that pulsing vein the way weathermen trusted Doppler radar.

"If you're fine, then put this on," Lois dared, picking up the blood pressure cuff and separating the Velcro tabs. "Take your own pressure and let's see."

Rebecca stepped inside, but only so she could speak privately. "Never mind that. I confess his tone rubbed me the wrong way," she admitted. "Like fingernails scratching a blackboard, actually. But I mean it, I'm not giving him the pleasure of getting to me. Maybe I'll even drop a curtsy as I go in."

"Oh, cripes," Lois fretted. "Everybody buckle up, we're going to get some turbulence."

"You'll see—I mean it. Cool and professional."

However, her resolve was under assault from the first moment she stepped into the doctor's private office.

Usually he prefaced his little lectures with attempts at polite small talk. This morning, however, he waded right in without even testing the water.

"Miss O'Reilly, last Friday I noticed you being extremely rude, in my opinion, with the sales rep from Med-Tech Supplies."

"I doubt if it left him a broken man," she countered, surprising herself at the sarcasm in her tone.

John Saville stared at her for a moment, not sure whether he or the salesman was the target of her scornful tone.

Both of us, he decided, and he felt his angry pulse thrum in his palms.

She's got a hell of a mouth on her, he fumed. But when he glanced at the defiant pout of her lips, he suddenly wondered what it would be like to kiss that angry mouth, kiss it hard until the anger turned to something very different....

Fat chance he had of ever finding out. That was obvious in the way she always looked at him as if she'd love to slap him.

"Yes?" she asked, cutting impatiently into his reverie, trying to get him back on track. "You saw me being rude, as you call it, with the Med-Tech guy?"

Her bossy tone irritated him anew. "Yeah, and now this morning," he forged on, "I learn that you've switched our account to Rocky Mountain Medical Supplies."

So that's what's got him all bent out of shape, she thought, noticing how his features seemed etched in anger.

"I didn't attempt to conceal the change from anyone," she countered, her face coolly indifferent to his obvious irritation. "Is there a problem?"

"None that *I* was aware of. That's precisely my point in asking. Why fix what isn't broken?"

"Rocky Mountain Medical is a dependable supplier. I switched for a good reason."

Those deep, intensely blue eyes cut into her like diamond drill bits. "That reason being...?"

The salesman was a married man hitting on me, that's why, she wanted to toss in his face. But she feared he would use it as proof of more "unprofessional behavior" on her part. Her resolve to rise above any fray crumbled completely. She suddenly flushed, more angry than embarrassed. "My reasons are personal."

"Yes," he said, smug with triumph, "I figured as much from your behavior last Friday. I could tell there was...something between the two of you."

"You can't possibly conclude—"

She caught herself in the nick of time before exploding. If this was just a fishing expedition, a search for things to throw in her face, she had no intention of taking his hook.

"Look," she told him, her hands balled into fists on her hips, "you know that it's the nurse in any office who uses most of the disposable medical supplies. Dr. Winthrop always trusted me—"

"Yeah, right, I know the riff by now," he said, cutting her off impatiently. "Paul Winthrop is God Almighty, and I'm the heartless outsider. The spawn of Satan."

His rather childish outburst surprised her. His tone had sounded almost human. She might even have felt some sympathy for him if she hadn't still felt the sting of his "your behavior last Friday" remark.

Not that it was any of his damn business, she fumed. Why not just call her the office slut and at least be a man about it instead of dropping smug hints like some little schoolyard snitch?

"I'm sorry," she told him archly, "that you feel so persecuted in Mystery, Doctor. I suppose we hayseed types must seem a bit quaint to sophisticated outsiders."

Her tone heaped extra emphasis on the last two words.

He wanted to laugh out loud. Staring at her, he thought, you beautiful, hotheaded little fool, you are so wrong it's even funny. Sophisticated? He almost snorted. What would she think if she knew he grew up living in a broken-down trailer, or that pretty girls just like her used to mock him in school because of his family's poverty? Medical school had been the only way out. The only way. And he'd grasped it like a lifebuoy.

But it hardly mattered what he thought. She didn't give him a chance to slip a word in.

"I am the office nurse, after all," she said, pushing right on in spite of his closed, angry glower. "It's my job to order medical supplies. But if you have some specific complaint about Rocky Moun—"

"No, it's fine, what the hell," he cut in sarcastically. "I'm only the doctor around here, don't let *me* interfere with your plans for the office."

"I said if you want, I'll order—"

"Order it from a Hong Kong clearing house for all I care," he snapped, his tone brusquely dismissive. "You're right, it's your job, not mine. Thanks for your time."

He sat down behind his desk and flipped open the current issue of *Surgical Medicine Quarterly*. His rude behavior was meant to be her dismissal.

But Rebecca saw how his eyes were not really reading. Anger flicked in his gaze like light reflected off midnight ice, darkening the blue and tightening his lips and facial muscles.

The feeling is mutual, her own angry eyes assured him right back as she turned away, resenting him to the point of pure hatred.

"One last thing, Miss O'Reilly."

His voice behind her stopped her like a firm grip on her shoulders.

She turned to watch him from the doorway of the office. "Yes?"

"Concerning what I witnessed last Friday—your, uh, personal intrigues are of course your own business. But *professionals* don't mix business with pleasure for this very reason we see now—it causes unnecessary problems. Try to keep your love life out of the workplace."

His presumptions and false assumptions made anger surge up within her, anger tinged with bewilderment. Why should she care if he had a false impression of her involvement with a would-be adultering creep? She refused to let Saville get that personal with her, right or wrong in his assumptions. His nose wasn't just out of joint—it was also way too long.

The scornful twist of her mouth was meant to insult him more than any words could. Nonetheless, she flung a few at him for good measure.

"Despite your obvious belief that you are above everyone else," she snipped, "this is not the Middle Ages, and you do not own your employees. I am a nurse, not a serf. My private life is my business and my business alone. Furthermore, as far as I see it, you have no right to make ridiculous observations like you have just now. In fact, you don't have the right to even speak to me about my love life."

Or lack thereof, she finished silently to herself with a twist of irony.

In the ensuing silence, her eyes refused to flee from his. Defiance edged every feature as she stared back at him.

His gaze turned toward the window and the view outside as if in surrender, but he still took up the gauntlet.

"If I did own you," he assured her, "I'd see if I could swap you for an angry grizzly. Might make the office more pleasant."

Down-home humor, she thought. Just what Mystery needed in a doctor from Chicago.

She turned and left the office. She didn't make note of his angry stare or how it drilled into her. Burning. Burning.

By the time Hazel McCallum left for her 10:00 a.m. appointment with John Saville, not even a sweater was required, and the main yard and corral were teeming with horse wranglers and cow punchers.

Weather-rawed men wearing range clothes and neckerchiefs waved as her cinnamon-and-black Fleetwood wound through the crushed-stone driveway of the front yard. Some of the older hands refused to wave, considering that gesture beneath their dignity and Hazel's status as the last living McCallum. Instead they touched their hats in a respectful "salute to the brand," a gesture that never ceased to make Hazel feel pride in the cattleman's traditions.

Those corporate boys in the big cities only talk about teamwork, she thought. One old-fashioned cattle drive would teach them the real meaning of pulling together.

She slowed for the asphalt road that led due east into town. Beyond the Lazy M's far-flung corrals and pastures, blue sky curved down to meet green grass in a vista as wide as the eye could see. And rising majestically beyond the verdant floor of Mystery Valley, the hard granite peaks of the Rockies.

Even the stunning view, however, couldn't quite keep her from remembering her daily horoscope, which she always consulted over morning coffee. She smiled, pleased but not at all surprised, as she recalled the advice to "make some connections that appear illogical on the surface."

Illogical? It was worse than that—Hazel knew Rebecca O'Reilly and John Saville might be her most challenging match yet. But at age seventy-five she was one of the last true mavericks in the American West. Oil money had subdued most of the cattle hierarchy, but the Lazy M brand had survived, even thrived, under her astute management.

And *she* thrived on a challenge—life was too flat without long shots and lost causes.

She wound through a curve, swooped across a little stone bridge, and now came in sight of the white-painted fence where her land gave way on its east border to John Saville's recently purchased property. She still thought of it as the Papenhagen place even though Tilly's husband had passed away last year and she had sold out, moving to South Florida to join the condo-and-blue-rinse set.

Hazel had always liked the big fieldstone house with its indestructible slate roof and windows with leaded panes.

The place is too big, though, for a bachelor, she thought yet again. It needed a wife, some dogs and cats, a few or a bunch of kids. If there were too many, she'd gladly handle the overflow, for Hazel missed having young neighbors around all the time as Rebecca and her school friends used to be, bless their hearts. If only kids wouldn't grow up so fast.

Seeing the house reminded her: Rebecca was wrong about the young surgeon's personality. Hazel was sure of that already, despite the fact he was not one to volunteer much about his past.

But she also knew that telling Rebecca about her mistake would be pointless. The girl was too headstrong, too young and independent. She would need to make the discovery on her own—with some guidance, of course, Hazel admitted to herself, from the area's best matchmaking operative. For she was nearly convinced, even this early on, that newcomer John Saville and hometown girl Rebecca were an ideal match. If only each could survive the mutual shell shock of their first impressions.

"Lord," Hazel said under her breath, "I'd be a hypocrite if I called matchmaking my burden. It's too much fun. I've never been bashful about meddling."

After all, she had some right to meddle. Her ancestors had been the first to settle in Mystery Valley; now she was determined to save as much of its traditional character as she could. That meant the careful pairing of natives with outsiders, forming bonds of real community. Bonds of real love.

John Saville's classic Alfa Romeo Gran Sport, painted bloodred in the Italian racing tradition, sat in his reserved spot beside the clinic. The very sight of it stirred Hazel's blood, for it had all the grace and power of a fine Thoroughbred. She parked in the spot beside it, admiring the graceful roadster body with its tan leather driver's seat mounted almost over the rear axle.

Not the car of choice for an ''old sobersides,'' she thought as she followed a cobblestone walk toward the glassed-in foyer.

''Sorry if I'm late, ladies,'' Hazel announced as she entered the waiting room. ''I spent too much time gawking at the tourists downtown. My land, *where* do they learn to dress like they do? They must have one of those whatcha-majiggers, a chat room for it on the Internet.''

All three of them usually poked harmless fun at the warm-weather influx of visitors, which grew larger every year. This morning, however, only Lois laughed with her. Rebecca was in one of her little snits that Hazel recognized well. Her pretty smile was in place, as usual, dazzling enough to fool most people. But the normally gentle and pleasing brow was now furled from pent-up anger. And that vein in her temple was pulsing, a sure sign.

Sensing Rebecca's mood, Lois took over. ''Hi, Hazel. You can come right on back if you want. I've got Becky's station set up.''

Instead of heading right to examination room A, Hazel paused between the two women's desks. ''You and your new boss getting along any better?'' she inquired bluntly of Rebecca.

''Oh, hey, better watch what you say,'' she replied in a sarcastic warning tone. ''The walls have ears, you know. Maybe even bugs planted in them.''

''I take it that's a no?''

''A big, loud, resounding no. Frankly, I think there're some people who took their toilet training *way* too seriously.''

''Takes one to know one,'' Hazel suggested sweetly.

''I'll pretend you didn't say that. You'll see. Don't be surprised if I'm reading the Help Wanted ads soon. I'm glad this guy doesn't wear a ring or we'd all have to kiss it.''

"Ahh-hemm." Lois, busy opening mail, cleared her throat, warning Rebecca to hold her voice down. But she was still smarting from her earlier encounter with the doctor and didn't much care what he overheard. Besides, in her mind Hazel was family, not a patient.

Hazel knew this headstrong side of her friend, had even encouraged it after a fashion when she saw how her mother's death left the poor girl faltering in her self-confidence. So Hazel also knew that the only way to handle the lass was with reverse psychology.

In short, she decided with a perverse little grin, maybe Becky needed a date from hell to remind the haughty princess what it's like "out there." And then John Saville might start to look a tad better to her.

"What are you smiling about?" Rebecca challenged her as she led her patient into the examination room.

"Oh, I'm just building castles in the air," Hazel confessed as she rolled up the sleeve of her blouse. "And even populating them."

"Hmm," was Rebecca's only comment. Anger still distracted her.

She checked Hazel's blood pressure and heart rate and recorded them on the chart in her clipboard. Next she took her temperature, then weighed her on the same old but reliable triple-beam scale Doc Winthrop had used for decades.

"Hazel," she remarked, impressed as usual, "you never vary by an ounce, do you?"

"Wouldn't know," Hazel admitted. "We McCallums never kept a scale around. What for? Your horse is the only one needs to worry about your weight."

A moment later John Saville appeared in the doorway, trim and handsome in gray slacks and a light-blue dress shirt with a navy rep tie, loosened but not sloppy. Rebecca handed him the clipboard and then stepped out, closing the door behind her and never once meeting his eyes.

"How've you been doing, Hazel?" he greeted her, friendly but somewhat distracted in his manner—just as Rebecca had been.

They've been at each other's throats, all right, the matriarch mused. No good romance should have bland beginnings.

"Feisty as ever," she assured him, "thanks to my talented young surgeon."

John pinched the creases of his trousers and tugged them up a fraction, taking over Rebecca's still-warm chair.

Before he could ask her anything else, Hazel demanded, "What year's your Alfa? I'm guessing it's a '27?"

His face changed immediately, the stern features softening, and enthusiasm lifted his tone. "Hey, you're pretty close. Nineteen twenty-five Gran Sport 1750," he boasted like a proud papa. "It's a classic and then some. That model won every road race of its day. She's got a supercharged motor, all original. Even today I can push her up close to ninety-five."

"A 1925, huh?" Hazel winked at him. "Made the same year I was born."

He glanced briefly at her chart, then smiled. "Yeah, right. And both of you appear to be in excellent running order," he remarked, holding those intensely blue eyes steady on her—more curious than suspicious, she decided. "I see you take only one medication?"

She nodded. "Nitroglycerin tablets. I only take them occasionally for mild angina pain."

"But didn't you mention to Miss O'Reilly—"

Her laugh cut him off. "Is it too hard to say Rebecca?"

"—to Rebecca that you had some questions about your diet since the surgery? Has there been some problem?"

"You know, I recall that I did mention something like that," she confessed, "but here's a better question just popped into my head—have you ever watched a cat sitting beside a gopher hole?"

The crease between his eyebrows deepened in a surprised frown. "Can't say that I have. I was a military brat, lived all over the world. Including near gopher holes. Don't remember any cats sitting beside them, though."

"Well, come on out to my place sometime, I've got cats *and* gopher holes," she assured him. "It's well worth watching. You'll soon learn that the cat's patience is surpassed only by one thing—its confidence that the wait is worth it."

He met her sparkling gaze for at least five seconds, and he suddenly realized, full force, that he was in the company of an extraordinarily perceptive person.

"There's a lesson for me in that, right?"

Indeed there was, but Hazel knew she had to give the good doctor his medicine in doses. He wouldn't admit it yet because he was still in the throes of denial. But he was "gone" on Rebecca, all right. Or not yet gone, she corrected herself, but he was going, going...and soon *would* be gone.

Right now he was still too irritated at her, baffled by her, his confidence thwarted because she was new to his experience. So during this visit, Hazel settled for merely planting a seed. She could water it later. Her secret garden of love.

"A lesson?" she finally responded, her tone innocent of any guile. "Why, Dr. Saville, I may not be the sharpest knife in the drawer, but no one ever has much trouble getting my point, if you'll excuse the pun. Well, my goodness!"

She glanced at her watch, then stood up.

John Saville hastily rose, too.

"I've got yard work to do," she explained. "The trees are still winter mulched, can you believe my lazy bones? And today I have to help pick out breed stock. Thanks for the wonderful advice."

"What advice? I didn't give you any."

"Well had you, I'm sure it would have been excellent advice."

"But, Hazel, we still haven't—"

"Toodle-oo," she called as she stepped quickly into the hallway. But she had more medicine to dispense before she left.

She deliberately left the door wide open so the doctor could hear her.

"Becky, hon," she called, her tone making it sound like a mere afterthought. "Do you remember Rick Collins, my accountant, Larry's, kid brother?"

Rebecca, busy taking inventory in the medical supply room, poked her head out into the hallway. She gave Hazel a little frown as she tried to recall. "Have I met him?"

"Not exactly, I don't believe. You saw him waiting in Larry's car one day in my driveway. Remember? You asked me who the cute guy was?"

Rebecca kept the blank expression as memory failed her. "I'm not sure I remember..."

"You said he had a nice smile. Sure you did. So I gave him your phone number," Hazel supplied in an offhand tone. "Suggested he give you a call soon. And I warned him not to put it off too long or he'd end up on the waiting list."

"Hazel," she protested, "I really don't remember—"

"Oh, Larry says he's loads of fun," Hazel said, cutting her off, already letting herself out. "He reads a lot, and you've always liked guys who read."

"Hazel, I can't—"

"I'll send a check when I get home," Hazel commented

to Lois as she closed the door behind her. Her last glimpse showed John Saville in the hallway, watching Rebecca with the same hard expression he usually wore around her.

Let not your hearts be troubled, youngsters, she reflected as she walked to her car. True love always finds a way.

Or at least a good agent, she added, and sheer deviltry sparkled in her Prussian-blue eyes.

Three

Rick Collins must have followed Hazel's advice about not wasting time, for he called later that very day. The phone rang only minutes after Rebecca had returned to her studio apartment, located just south of Mystery on Bluebush Road. Her place was only minutes from Valley General Hospital, where she'd worked as a surgical-recovery nurse briefly before Dr. Winthrop hired her, impressed by colleagues' reports about her work.

Her very first telephone impression of Rick had been favorable. A nice voice, decidedly masculine but not macho, and he identified himself immediately. No cute little guessing games like some guys played. He simply skipped any preliminaries and politely asked her to dinner the coming weekend at the Hathaway House.

He was a bit businesslike and direct about it, but she sort of liked his confident, why-don't-we-close-a-deal manner, so she accepted. He was friendly without sounding desperate or nervous in the way of men who placed *too* much importance on a date. And the Hathaway House in nearby Summerfield, while no leader in trendy cuisine, was generally considered the best restaurant in Mystery Valley— respectable but hardly formidable, appropriate for a safe first date.

She had hung up the phone feeling better than she usually did after making a blind date. Well, not actually a *totally* blind date, she reminded herself while she washed and rinsed a few dirty plates and set them in the drainer. After all, she finally remembered who the guy was. She'd gotten a good look at Rick once a few months ago from Hazel's kitchen window.

She recalled his collar-length blond hair and the gorgeous, sexy smile he'd flashed at her when he caught her scoping him out from the window. But Rick had been at least four or five years ahead of her in school, so she'd never met him and knew little about him except that he was still single and worked for a manufacturing company located about fifteen miles from Mystery.

She was perhaps a little bothered by his by-the-book manner. She liked to flirt a little, but he had passed up the opportunities she had given him over the phone.

God forbid that he'd turn out to be another John Saville—just a good-looking vinyl boy who reserved his charm for debutantes and Vassar grads.

Something else bothered her about the brief conversation. Hazel had implied that she knew Rick well. Yet he admitted on the phone he hardly knew her. But so what if Hazel was being a little pushy. The old girl had always seen herself as a crusader in the cause of romance. Had some notable successes at it, too.

Romance... Rebecca rinsed her hands, then used her wet fingers to comb back a few rebellious strands of chestnut hair that had escaped the barrettes. Suddenly the old rumination came to her again: for too long now she'd been wondering what "doing it" was really like. She'd been close a few times with Brian, but something had always stopped her—some inner sense that the time just wasn't right. In Brian's case, it was the commitment that wasn't right; she saw that now. She only hoped that the next time she had the opportunity to take the plunge, her instincts would go away. So far they'd only prevailed in keeping her from making any move. And she was tired of her virginity, and getting cynical.

If she couldn't find love, then she at least wanted to pretend she knew about it.

Unbidden, an image of John Saville's intense cobalt eyes, raking over her like fingers, filled the screen of her mind, and a restless yearning stirred low in her stomach, quickening her pulse.

That's just great, she chided herself—a cute guy just asked you out, and here you are fantasizing about some self-loving, elitist snob who wouldn't be caught dead with you in public.

Another doctor in her life might send her screaming for the nunnery. So she erased the unwanted image of John Saville from her mind and returned to drying the dishes.

Surprisingly, the rest of the week went by smoothly at the clinic, as if John Saville were on his best behavior. Late on Friday afternoon he came up front from his private office.

"Ladies," he announced in his stilted, formal manner, "I've finished reviewing Dr. Winthrop's financial books. I see that neither of you has received a raise in almost two years now."

His fiercely blue eyes lingered on Rebecca, seeming to dwell on the spots where a snug cashmere pullover, despite her bra, clearly marked her nipples. He cleared his throat.

"So I've informed our bookkeeper," he continued, "that retroactive from the day I took over, you both are to receive a 10 percent raise. Also three more paid personal-leave days."

Rebecca was too pleasantly surprised to speak.

Lois, however, quickly thanked him on behalf of them both. They received a second shock when John Saville actually flashed a quick and very charming smile—nothing imperious about it.

"Nonsense, both of you earn your salaries," he insisted.

He left, taking some mail with him back to his office.

Lois looked at Rebecca, then fanned herself with the folder in her hand, as if bringing down her temperature.

"Sexy smile. And does that man look good in herringbone dress slacks? Especially from the *rear.*"

But a moment later she added, "A pox on myself for such adulterous thoughts. And me the property of the Gang of Four." The Gang of Four was Lois's name for her husband, Merrill, and their three sons, who ran Brubaker and Sons Automotive in nearby Colfax.

She looked at Rebecca before adding, "Besides, he was putting the eye on *you,* Miss O'Reilly. Oo-la-la."

Rebecca was unimpressed. "I wouldn't alert the media if I were you, because I doubt that. Unless the doctor had a brief fantasy about slumming with the scullery help."

"You ingrate. The man just padded our pay envelopes. And you saw how sweet he was about it."

"I appreciate the raise," she told Lois. "But he's right, we are due for one, girlfriend."

"Not to mention well worth it," Lois conceded. "Lutheran Hospital has been wooing you ever since you did your nursing practicum there. And I'll have my business degree in another year—I know for a fact Bruce Everett wants to hire me to manage his new dude ranch."

Rebecca only half heard her friend, thinking about John

Saville. "If you ask me," she speculated, lowering her voice, "he's one of these big carrot-and-stick commandos. This raise is a carrot meant to bring us—*me,* actually—into line."

"And when he gets that uptight look like somebody's giving him a wedgie," Lois giggled, "that's one of the sticks."

They enjoyed a rebellious laugh. Their goof-off mood inspired Rebecca to suddenly pucker her face in an exaggerated scowl.

"'Having fun, Miss O'Reilly,'" she lectured, making her voice as deep and disapproving as she could, "'isn't the point of this clinic.'"

They were safe, for he was well out of earshot at the rear of the building. However, the sudden sound of his steps in the hallway caught them before they could quite suppress their mood of bubbling mirth.

"Shush, woman," Lois hissed melodramatically. "We just got a raise, don't get him mad."

But that last smart crack was one joke too many, and badly timed. She had to swivel sideways in her chair, and Lois barely managed to compose her face before the doctor appeared in the doorway, several X-rays in his left hand.

"Miss O'Reilly, has the lab got back with us yet on Bernie Decker's blood-and-urine workups?"

His request was polite and straightforward, similar to dozens he made each day.

Rebecca never would have foolishly lost it if she hadn't made the dumb mistake of making eye contact with Lois so soon after they'd just been goofing around.

It was the "Miss O'Reilly" that did it—it was like a spark to a powder keg.

"Yes, Doctor," was all she managed before she lost her composure and broke into giggles that set Lois off, too.

For a few moments after their adolescent outburst, he

was caught completely off guard. Rebecca watched a perplexed smile draw his lips apart. At first he seemed to think something else was causing their mirth. Then she saw a quick glimmer of realization in his eyes that *he* was the butt of the joke. Then his face registered some deeper emotion—hurt, she realized with a sudden stab of guilt. They were only being immature and laughing at his stuffy formality, but he couldn't know that.

An indrawn, bitter look came over him, and the handsome, angry face closed against both of them.

"All right," he replied, still under control but so mad that his jaw muscles bunched tightly. "I guess I'll get that lab report later, when you two've gotten over your private joke."

Guilt gnawed at Rebecca for the rest of the day. It wasn't just her childish behavior and the raise thing—she thought of John Saville's brief but charming smile, the hurt deep in his eyes before anger took over. She also thought about how his gaze had seemed to linger on her body. Not that she cared. No doubt the lover within him was as uptight and calculating as the physician. Being with him wouldn't be worth the enormous effort she'd have to put forth just to have some fun.

However, all her guilt was whisked away like a feather in a gust the moment she tried to apologize right before quitting time at 5:00 p.m.

He cut her off in midsentence with almost the same caustic retort she had recently flung at him. "I doubt it will leave me a broken man."

And to think she had wasted time feeling sorry for such an overbearing brute. The absolute creep, she fumed as she drove home in the aging but reliable Bronco her father had turned over to her as a high school graduation present. He was so like Brian. His spitting image exactly, she told herself, self-justification in every word.

Even thoughts of her upcoming date tonight with Rick Collins could not crowd irksome images of John Saville from her mind.

By the time she finished a long and relaxing bath, the light of late afternoon was taking on the mellow richness just before sunset. Wearing a snug terry cloth robe, her long hair wrapped in a towel, she watched the copper blaze of sunset from her bedroom window.

Feeling calmer, she dressed in a hunter green merino wool skirt and a black silk blouse, digging a good pair of black leather pumps out of her closet. She left her hair unrestrained, just combing it out and spritzing it back a little in front, letting it cascade down her back and over her shoulders.

"A very sexy little package," she approved as she checked herself out in the full-length mirror on the back of the bathroom door. "Play your cards right, Mr. Collins, and who knows? This girl is *in the mood.*"

She hummed pop tunes while she added a finishing touch, a pair of delicate cameo pierced earrings that had belonged to her mother. But while she slipped the delicate French wires through her ears, again she saw John Saville's face closing against her, the intense cobalt eyes accusing.

A little guilt, and plenty of anger, knotted her stomach, already pinched with hunger.

He was the last man she wanted on her mind tonight.

Noticing it was almost seven o'clock, she quickly opened her compact and lightly brushed her cheeks with blush, trying to get in the right mindset to enjoy a date, John Saville be damned.

Rick Collins rang her doorbell at 7:00 p.m., prompt as a wake-up call and looking quite dapper in a dark evening suit. His blond hair was shorter and neater than she recalled, and he was a little stouter than she had imagined him. Nonetheless, he made a good first impression when Rebecca opened the door.

The smile was still as sexy as she remembered it being. Definitely movie-star teeth.

She was a little put off, however, when he escorted her out to his vehicle: a glittering gold SUV that rode incredibly high off the ground on huge, oversize tires.

"Not quite a monster truck." Rick seemed to apologize as he helped her in.

She felt as if she was climbing up into a military assault vehicle. This is Montana, she reminded herself. People drive weird trucks out here.

But from that point on, the date rapidly became a fiasco.

During the drive to the restaurant, he rebuffed her every attempt at conversation because, as she quickly learned, he was obsessed with reciting trivial facts. Batting averages, team mascots, per capita consumption of chocolate, the cures for diphtheria in Colonial America, an endless, random recitation of pointless facts proving he had a photographic memory but no other apparent intelligence. Hazel was right to call him a big reader, but she failed to mention he read nothing but books on trivia.

Before long she had also noticed something quite irritating about Rick's "pleasant voice"—it was oddly uniform in tone, seldom varying much. He might as well be reading out loud from a phone book to pass time. The monotony of it had quickly begun to grate on her.

The date officially tanked by the time the Hathaway House loomed into view. She was practically clawing at her window to escape. He hadn't shut up once.

"No kidding," his monotone voice droned on like a weed-eater idling, "Charles Bronson was actually named Charles Buchinsky before he changed his name."

"Is that right?" she muttered.

"Yeah, and John Denver was Henry John Deutschen-dorf, Jr. And you know what Eric Clapton's real name was?"

"You tell me."

He laughed for the first time. "Eric Clap. No kidding, it really was."

When she said nothing, he pressed on. "Don't you get—"

"I get it," she answered, wondering how she was going to get through the interminable two hours of dinner.

The modern exterior of the Hathaway House, with its elegant marble walls, seemed a deliberate contrast to the old-time intimacy of the interior. Candles burned in sconces along the walls, and two-branched gilt candlesticks illuminated each table.

But tonight it was all wasted on Rebecca. The double line of full-length windows opening onto a scrolled-iron balcony, the tables bright and fragrant with fresh bouquets of spring—all wasted.

In fact even as a pallid and bored maître d' escorted them to their tables, it was all she could do to restrain herself from bolting. She still smarted with humiliation from their arrival—she had actually required a valet's help to climb down out of Rick's truck.

"Hopalong Cassidy's horse was Topper," Rick's voice hammered on, beating at her ears by now. "Dale Evans rode Buttermilk, the Cisco Kid was on Diablo, Gene Autry rode—"

I dared to dream, Rebecca thought with self-lacerating sarcasm that made her smile. Unfortunately she was looking right at Rick when she did it. His next remark proved he misread her ironic smile as some sort of romantic green light.

"I thought maybe after dinner," he confided in a near whisper so others wouldn't hear, "we might take a little ride out to Turk Road."

He couldn't be serious. Cold revulsion made her shudder. Turk Road used to be a local lovers' lane until huge feed-lots were built on both sides of it. Either he hadn't parked there in a long time or he didn't care about the smell.

"You're joking, right?" she blurted out. "That area smells like a leaking sewer."

"Oh, not when the wind's out of the north," he assured her with a solemn face. "Like it is tonight. We can just keep the windows rolled up."

They were seated, and immediately the wine steward hovered at Rick's elbow while he ordered some white zin-fandel she had no intention of drinking.

A brief image of Rick groping her in his almost-monster truck, windows steamed over, cows bellowing on all sides, had killed her earlier appetite.

"Take me home," she blurted out suddenly. "I don't feel well."

"What? But we—"

"I really *don't* feel well," she insisted in a tone that quashed any further resistance from him. To underline her determination she stood up and gathered her purse and sweater.

"Man, oh, man!" he exclaimed in frustration. "Hazel didn't tell me you were such a dingbat."

Well at least he gets angry, she thought as the two of them walked quickly outside, scrutinized by curious eyes.

"The gold truck," Rick snapped to the valet, and the latter trotted around to the side lot. The teen returned a minute later, shaking his head at them.

"Bad news, sir. Your right rear tire is completely flat. If you've got a jack that's big enough, we'll change it for you."

Rebecca's heart sank at this stroke of rotten luck, and Rick cursed. "No, it'll have to be towed to a hoist. Or at least lifted by a tow-truck winch."

He looked at Rebecca as if it were all her fault. "I'll have to call a tow. Looks like it'll be a while before you get home."

The date from hell, she thought, as she watched him walk away with the valet to inspect the damage.

Four

Oh, great, Rebecca groaned inwardly while her date dug the phone number for his tow service out of his wallet. Mystery Valley had virtually no cab service, just a shuttle bus service for the airport at Helena, so she couldn't get home that way.

Hazel...her place wasn't all that far, or maybe Lois—

A low rumble of exhaust and a flash of bright-red paint pulled her attention to the street out front. John Saville, looking handsome and slightly windblown in a brown leather bomber jacket, parked his Gran Sport classic right out front and leaped athletically out without opening the door. He carried his leather medical kit and hurried toward the restaurant, ignoring the valets.

"Got it," Rick muttered beside her, finally finding the number. He had already retrieved the wireless phone from his vehicle. "Shouldn't be too long," he told her, avoiding her eyes now. "It doesn't make sense I'd have a flat, those are brand-new tires."

She stood there on the sidewalk, her irritation at herself tinged with sudden curiosity. She wondered what emergency could possibly have called John Saville to the restaurant. The place had seemed calm enough when she and Rick came outside.

An inexplicable flat tire and the doctor's sudden arrival—certainly it was odd timing.

Rick finished his call and pushed down the antenna of his phone. "Forty minutes to an hour," he informed her.

She resisted the urge to snap at him in frustration. It wasn't his fault, after all. "I think I'll go inside and see if I can call a—"

"Rebecca!"

The voice cut into her thoughts. She turned around. John Saville went toward her, dressed in stone-washed jeans and a white pullover she could see under his open jacket.

He actually used my first name, she thought.

Evidently, however, he had not approached her to be friendly. His tight-lipped smile of greeting seemed to cost him great effort.

"Dr. Saville," she greeted him. When he sent a quick glance at Rick she added with perfunctory politeness, "Rick Collins, this is my employer, Dr. John Saville."

"Excuse me for butting in, both of you, but I wonder if you know anything about an elderly woman who had a dizzy spell inside the restaurant? I got the call a few minutes ago, but no one inside seems to know a thing about it."

Rebecca thought once again, How odd. Her suspicions grew stronger. Everyone knew Hazel had matchmaking on her mind. But the town matriarch was tricky. It would be just like Hazel to pull a bait and switch. Accusation aimed squarely at Hazel niggled at her for a few seconds, but it passed as abruptly as it popped into her mind. She had too much to deal with right now to give it the consideration it deserved.

"I didn't notice any trouble," she replied. "Did you, Rick?"

He was still in a sullen mood since she had poured cold water on his hot plans for later.

"Maybe whoever it was left already," he suggested without interest.

"Well..." John Saville's gaze raked over Rebecca. He had never seen her with her hair unrestrained like this, framing her face.

"Well," he repeated, starting to turn away, "I guess it was a false alarm."

"Dr. Saville?"

Her voice brought him back around to face them. "Yes?"

Of all the people to request a favor from, why did it have to be him?

"I, that is, Rick's truck has a flat tire, and he has to wait for someone to come fix it. Could you—would you mind giving me a lift home? If it's not too far out of your way."

"Hey, whoa, here," Rick objected, sensing an invasion of his male territory. "This is still *my* date with you, not his."

The totally unwarranted possessiveness made her flush— she hardly knew the guy. He sure had a lot of nerve.

Despite her horror at making a public scene, she couldn't stop herself from saying, "If I could remind you, Rick, I'm not exactly feeling well, remember?"

"Look," the doctor said with diplomatic politeness, addressing himself to Rick, "there's a service station a few blocks down the street. Why don't I run the tire over there and get it patched?"

It irked her, suddenly, that her employer showed more consideration for this stranger than he did for her. He walks with kings, she thought scornfully, but never loses the common touch—until he comes to work.

Rick shook his head at the offer of help. "Even if we could get it off the vehicle, you'd need a truck to haul it."

John looked puzzled. Rick pointed out the towering vehicle. At the astonished look on her boss's face, Rebecca felt her cheeks heat.

She wanted to go crawl in a hole somewhere. "It's not *quite* a monster truck," she explained lamely, quoting Rick.

But by now John's politeness and gentlemanly deference toward her date had calmed Rick down. "Look, Doc," he said, "Rebecca says she doesn't feel well, and she'd like to go home. You'd be doing both of us a favor if you drove her, believe me."

"Glad to help."

Oh, that's great, she thought crossly. You two become blood brothers so I can look like the big bad witch. The doctor could treat a stranger's pride with such diplomacy, yet look how he acted toward his office nurse, as if her self-esteem meant less to him than killing a fly.

"Thank you, Rick," she said, feeling awkward.

He simply nodded and turned away, managing to make her feel guilty.

John Saville said nothing as the two of them approached his long, low-slung Alfa Romeo. But as he opened the passenger's door for her he said, "You really don't feel well?"

She settled into the low leather seat, sensing his gaze on her legs as her skirt rode up high. "It's what we women call a diplomatic headache."

"Ahh...medical school doesn't cover that one."

He went around, tossed the leather kit behind his seat, then got in and keyed the sports car to rumbling life. "Sorry it didn't work out," he told her. "He seems like a nice enough guy."

"Good," she retorted as he gunned away from the curb,

tires squealing. "You go out with him, then. You two sure seemed to hit it off."

She regretted her rudeness almost immediately. After all, he *was* giving her a lift home.

They were still in town, and overhead lights illuminated him well. She cast a sidelong glance as he accelerated through the gears, his hair whipping, right hand working the floor-mounted gearshift.

He caught her watching him.

"Nice jacket," she told him.

He shifted gears, and his hand brushed against her calf. Did it linger there a moment?

"My dad gave it to me," he replied.

"Was he a pilot in the military?"

A shadow seemed to cross his face, but it might have been something blocking the streetlights for a moment. "No," he replied curtly, adding nothing else, even though she waited.

He can't get personal with the lower class, she reminded herself sarcastically. Daddy was probably a big-time, four-star general, at least, judging from his son's arrogance.

He downshifted for the last traffic light in Summerfield. Again his hand brushed her leg. She really didn't have much room to move it. It was chilly in May after sunset, and she wore only a light sweater. When they stopped at the red light he shrugged out of his jacket and draped its comforting warmth over her shoulders.

"You don't have to—"

"You'll need it," he insisted, cutting her off. "I like to drive fast."

She quickly realized he meant what he said.

He was an excellent driver who appreciated the challenges of a winding road. The old Alfa Romeo roared through the star-speckled Montana night, flashing in and out of dark patches of moon shadow. They soared through dips that made Rebecca feel exciting loss-of-gravity tickles in her stomach.

Once outside the Summerfield limits, only the dash lights cast any illumination on them. She noticed how his taut forearm muscles leaped like machine cables each time he shifted—which he seemed to do a lot. And each time, his hand brushed her nyloned calf.

Again she told herself she really couldn't move in the cramped compartment. But in truth she liked the way the gearshift vibrated against her leg, the way the engine pulsed and throbbed through her soles, and the power surges of the accelerating motor were strangely thrilling, as was the increasingly electric contact of his fingers brushing her calf....

She caught herself just in time. She must shake off this erotic lull and curb such dangerous thoughts. She was still in her...excitable mood of earlier tonight, before Rick's onslaught of trivia had killed it. She mustn't forget this was not some hot fantasy man beside her, but Dr. Dry-As-Dust, surgical snob extraordinaire. She would only get into trouble wanting him. He would be just like Brian—thinking she was good enough to use but not good enough for forever.

Conversation was impractical in the engine roar and wind noise of the open road. But two miles west of Summerfield they got stuck behind a slow-moving logging truck.

Whether he's dry as dust or not, I still owe the guy an apology, she reminded herself. Again memory gave her a stab as she recalled how she and Lois had burst out laughing at him earlier today, how that nice smile died on his lips.

"Dr. Saville—"

"Please call me John. We aren't in the office." He snapped it out like an order, not a friendly request.

"John, Lois and I weren't sharing any private joke earlier today when we had our giggle attack. We were just in a silly mood."

"Look, if you're worried I'll change my mind about the raise, don't."

His curt, sarcastic tone made a storm of anger rise within her.

"That's what I get," she said in a voice caustic as acid, "for trying to be human with you."

His handsome jaw went slack with surprise at her peppery retort. But the remark had brought back his earlier humiliation. He had tried to meet her halfway, and she'd laughed in his face like he was a fool.

He clamped his teeth rather than tell her what he felt like saying.

They finally got a clear stretch of road, and he flew past the logging truck, exhaust roaring. His fast, angry driving suited Rebecca's mood, too.

The silence also gave her a chance to reconsider her earlier suspicion. A date arranged by Hazel, a suddenly flat tire, a supposed emergency phone call for the doctor...

"Which way?" His curt voice cut into her thoughts as they reached the town limits of Mystery.

"Go through town then turn right on Bluebush Road," she told him. "It's the Sagewood Apartments, a couple miles out of town."

Minutes later he braked to a skidding stop in front of her building and waited impatiently, motor running, for her to shrug out of his jacket and get out. He refused to help her out, and the race car had not been designed to accommodate women in skirts. With all the grace of a truckload of bricks, she managed to get her feet outside and stood up.

The big arc-sodium yard light was on, and she could feel his eyes on her. Her clothes needed "a good pull-down" as her aunt Thelma used to call it.

"Thanks for the ride."

"It's on my way," he assured her, his tone implying that's the only reason he did it.

A moment later he gunned the motor, and she watched ruby-red taillights head back out toward the road.

John welcomed the feel of crisp night air stinging his fresh-shaven cheeks. It helped to cool his body, which still burned from the contact with Rebecca's leg every time he shifted—that and the image of her rich, lustrous chestnut mane framing the face of an innocent wanton....

With her heartbreak smile, Rebecca O'Reilly was the most beautiful woman he had ever seen. But it didn't matter because no matter how much he'd heard about her sense of humor, her spirit, even her optimistic heart, she'd shown him none of it.

In the dim light of his car he had seen in her eyes how she hated him.

Detested him might be a better word. *Hate* implied a level of emotional interest she could not possibly feel for him. And she'd detested him from their first meeting. Detested him probably because he wasn't laid-back and informal like her precious Paul Winthrop or the other men she was used to. Because he didn't joke around on the job. Her contempt angered him, and it only made him angrier trying to figure out why he cared at all.

And *why* did he have to mention his father to her? A pilot—what irony. His father bought him the jacket out of guilt over all the childhood beatings. Woodrow Saville had ended up a failure in his enlisted military career, never rising above the rank of sergeant and eventually drummed out of the Army early for poor conduct-and-proficiency reports. The best he could provide for his family was a trailer next to the Bitterroot Valley dump.

And he had taken all his failures out on his only son.

Despite the fact John was an outstanding student and athlete—or maybe because of that—his father treated him like a perpetual loser who screwed up everything he tried to do.

He remembered the commanding cadence of his father's stern voice, an ironic warning from one of life's big losers: *Failure is not an option, John, and only weak men need to be liked.* Despite his contempt for his father, he had been forced to live up to those hard words. And despite all his success as a surgeon, the early emotional scars remained.

But neither his pride nor his father's indoctrination could quell the image of Rebecca pushing her hair out of her eyes, or that quick glimpse he got of her long, shapely legs. He was acutely aware of his body's need for a woman. He hadn't slept with one since he'd been out here, although a few had already made it clear that fact could easily change.

Too bad none of them was wicked, wild, teasing Rebecca. Just a flash of her eyes sent a hunger that gnawed to his spine. It was becoming more and more difficult to accept her rejection of him and contemplate another woman.

He hit a stretch of empty, open road and floored the gas pedal, feeling his Alfa surge like a powerful beast.

At least, he reminded himself, this was an off weekend for him. Tomorrow he'd put Mystery in his rearview mirror and spend two full days where he knew he was welcome and appreciated.

He was grateful for the distraction of his secret weekends. Who knows, he thought, with luck he might even get Rebecca O'Reilly out of his mind for a while.

One thing, however, was sure. She'd be on his mind tonight, all right, and if he was lucky, she'd be much nicer to him in his dreams.

* * *

"What in Sam Hill are you doing at *home?*" Hazel demanded when Rebecca called her at nine-thirty. "And alone? You and Rick should still be eating dessert."

"We never got to dessert," Rebecca assured her, placing ironic emphasis on the last word. "In fact, we never even got into the main course. I just now popped some three-day-old quiche Lorraine into the microwave. I'm starving."

Hazel's voice took on a steel edge. "Don't tell me Rick stood you up, hon? If that—"

"Oh, heavens, Hazel, that would've been wonderful if he did that. The man's a walking trivia handbook. Did you know that?"

"Now you mention it," Hazel replied evasively, "maybe Larry said something about that."

"Maybe?" Rebecca repeated ironically, still suspecting that she'd been "wrangled" by a master rancher.

"Oh, it couldn't've been all that bad. It seems harmless enough, don't you enjoy a little escapism?"

"Hazel, I mean it, say anything and he starts spouting facts. But he's got no use whatsoever for a conversation, he's all boring monologue. I thought you said he was a lot of fun?"

"No, dear, I told you his brother Larry said that. Family loyalty, I guess."

"I s'pose," Rebecca agreed, not quite believing her friend but lacking any solid evidence against her. "Well, that's the last time I take an accountant's recommendation on romance. Hazel, are you sure this date was on the up-and-up?"

"Why, what's got into you?"

Briefly, Rebecca summed up the fiasco that ended in a flat tire and a ride home with John Saville.

"And I'll just bet," Hazel said, "that you were snotty with your boss, weren't you?"

For a moment Rebecca remembered his strong-jawed profile as he drove, felt his hand brushing her leg, the pulsing throb of the car's engine. It wasn't *him*, she thought crossly—the physical reactions to his nearness were just my body reminding me I've been a virgin for way too long now.

"I was rather…crisp with him, yes," she admitted. "But there's no other way to deal with him. I tried to be nice, and he jumped all over me. See? He's more like Brian than I could have imagined. I guess I'm just not upper-crust enough to deserve any respect. He treats me just the way all the other doctors—"

"Oh, phooey, Paul Winthrop didn't treat you that way, and you know it. I'm not one to love doctors, girl, 'cause at my age I go to way too many of 'em, but there's good in them. You just can't see it anymore because you got your heart broke."

Rebecca sighed. "Once burned—well, you know the phrase, Hazel. But I'm better off for the scars. Now I can see where I'm going to get into trouble, and John Saville is definitely the heartless type. There are way too many women chasing after him. And boy, can he turn on the charm when he wants to. You should have seen the grin he had on his face when Louise Wallant arrived one day. And she wasn't there for a physical, either. She strolled right into his private office and shut the door. I hear the whole town's burning up with gossip about the two of them—and they're a perfect match. She's just what I would have pictured for the 'real' Brian. She looks just right on Dr. Saville's arm, too."

"You're wrong, Rebecca. Why, even *you* said he jumped all over you."

"You know I didn't mean that literally." Rebecca rolled her eyes and smiled. "So I'll ignore that one. But, look, if he *likes* me now, I'd hate to get on his bad side."

"I'm not pushing you at him," Hazel assured her. "You're a big girl. You make up your own mind. But I don't expect a catch like him to be available forever."

"Oh, don't worry about that. He won't stay single long—the first eligible woman who's high enough in the social registry will snap him up. God knows plenty of them are finding excuses to come to the office."

After the slightest pause Hazel said, "From what I heard today at Selmer's Bakery, that may already have happened. A rich woman snapping him up, I mean."

Rebecca was surprised, then dismayed, at the keen sting of disappointment these words caused her.

"With whom?" she inquired, hoping her tone was casual.

"Louise Wallant, of course."

Louise Wallant…just hearing her name sent a bile taste into Rebecca's throat.

"Could be the same saloon gossip you heard, is all. But Edna Beck claims Louise is the reason he chose Mystery to practice medicine."

Rebecca recalled his angry words: *I didn't just stick a pin in the map. I picked this town.*

"Edna says John came to this area for a rock-climbing vacation while he was still in medical school. Claims he and Louise had a summer fling. But then, Edna's not one to worry how reliable her sources are. It could be a bunch of bull."

"If it is true, as I said before, they're the perfect match," Rebecca pronounced dismissively.

Louise was rich, pretty and spoiled rotten. All through high school she had tried to steal away any guy who showed interest in Rebecca, mainly to punish her for not joining the Louise Adoring Fan Club. But she was more than welcome to Dr. Dry-As-Dust, Rebecca tried to convince herself.

"Nonsense," Hazel scoffed at her. "I can believe the summer fling story, of course, considering Louise's looks and body. She's what my cowhands call 'a target of opportunity.' But John would never in a million years fall in love with her type. He has more sense than that."

"Fall in love? What, John Saville? Hazel, a golden boy does not succumb to passions. Mating is an investment strategy like—like—opening an IRA."

"Dear," Hazel's tone scolded, "you're way too young to be so bitter. You're turning into a grizzled old cynic."

"Don't forget I just barely survived a date tonight."

"I'll run my traps, dear, find out which good catches are out there. You'll see, we'll do better next time."

"Forget it. No more dating surprises for me, thanks. The next guy I date will submit a résumé and psychological profile tests."

Rebecca hung up feeling irritated and vaguely suspicious. Hazel bragged about being a Cupid, but tonight's dating disaster proved even Cupid could blow it in a big way. She owed Hazel a lot, but she would *not* be the lab rat for another experiment in wretched blind dates.

Soon, however, her irritation at Hazel gave way to unwelcome thoughts about Louise Wallant. The successful young entrepreneur maintained one house in Mystery, another in Deer Lodge, a tourist mecca nestled amidst beautiful national forests in some of the state's most pristine country. Her success in the bed-and-breakfast business, however, was not due so much to merit as to wealthy parents who constantly covered her financial butt.

Rebecca was sick to death of constantly hearing everyone around town talk about Louise this and Louise that as if she were a celebrity. All because she had a "perky" manner and one of those fake smiles as big as Texas—a smile that showed too many teeth, in Rebecca's opinion.

She ate a few bites of her by now lukewarm quiche, then

lost her appetite. She cleaned up in the kitchen before selecting a good novel and curling up on the sofa with a crocheted afghan draped over her shoulders.

However, it was no use. The words on the page kept squiggling out of focus as her thoughts were diverted.

She recalled one of the last things John Saville did today at the office. He changed the message on the answering machine, which usually gave his home phone number in case of emergencies. The new message said he'd be out of town all weekend and referred all calls to Dr. Brining in nearby Lambertville. He had told her and Lois, when he first took over his new practice, that he'd be out of town every other weekend "until further notice."

She had joked to Lois that he was probably sneaking away to be alone with a mirror. Now she couldn't help wondering if he was keeping a tryst with Louise.

"What do I care?" she said out loud, ignoring her novel. "Serves each of them right."

In fact she hoped they *were* an item: Dr. Dry-As-Dust and his toothy little profit princess. They could breed a bunch of perky and pretty little snobs to carry on their narcissism.

When it came to cattle breeds Hazel was sharp as a dagger. But when it came to judging men, Rebecca decided, Hazel was too easily tricked by a pleasing exterior. No question John Saville looked like a young Greek god. Unfortunately, like Dr. Brian Gage he had an ego far bigger than his heart.

Five

"Our young doctor looks plenty tuckered out," Lois confided to Rebecca shortly after the office had opened on Monday morning. "And he's got two surgeries scheduled today. Have you caught wind of the story Edna Beck's been peddling?"

Rebecca, busy preparing a pickup for the lab courier, only nodded. No doubt the John and Louise rumor had already raced through the valley. She tried not to succumb to a sudden flaring of irritation at yet another reminder that poor girls who drove used cars were not marriageworthy for the great doctor.

"Good," she retorted, not even bothering to lower her voice. "I hope they boffed like bunnies the entire weekend. Maybe that'll take some of the meanness out of him."

Lois, who was adding toner to the office printer, looked askance at her co-worker. Rebecca had been snappish and out of sorts ever since she arrived. Luckily John Saville's first patient today was Lauren Ulrick, a motormouth who never let anyone get in a word edgewise—even from the nearby exam room the doctor wouldn't likely overhear Rebecca's caustic barbs.

"Let me guess," Lois told the younger woman. "You had a disastrous date on Friday night?"

"Actually the entire weekend was a washout," Rebecca informed her. "All I got out of it was two days older."

"You can afford two days," Lois assured her. "To me you're still a junior miss. Just wait till you're staring down the road at forty, baby-cakes. It stares right back."

Yeah, Rebecca thought disconsolately.

At the rate she was going, she'd be the town's resident old maid by forty. She could just see her pathetic personal ad in *Valley Singles:* "Middle-aged virgin desperately seeks any more-or-less desirable man."

Lois studied her friend's preoccupied face and gave her an encouraging pat on the shoulder.

"Cheer up. Romance is a wheel of fortune—after it spins you down, it has nowhere to go but right back up."

"It sure takes a long time to revolve," Rebecca carped as she disappeared into the stock room to finish the quarterly drug inventory.

However, between entries on her clipboard, her mind kept returning to one thought like a tongue to a chipped tooth: John Saville on Friday night, the way he looked and moved and his manner with her—he had seemed almost...dangerous and exciting, far different from the humorless and rigid man she worked with.

Thinking of him, however, naturally brought her mind back to Louise Wallant. It was probably true about the two of them being involved. Involved in *what*—a casual affair or something more than that—she wasn't very clear about. Whatever it might be, it certainly wasn't her business. He had been very closemouthed to her and Lois about those weekends when he wouldn't be available, but that was his right. He had no business in her love life, and she had no business in his.

The talk means absolutely nothing to me, of course, she assured herself. It's just morbid curiosity. A lover's tryst twice a month...perhaps Louise would even have some other lover, too, for the doctor's off weeks. But Rebecca suspected twice a month just might be sufficient for a disciplined man like Dr. Saville.

And just how would you know, she chided herself, how much sex would be sufficient for anyone. Better to ask a duck about survival in the desert.

Across the hall the door to the examination room swung open.

"Mother always wanted me to be a model." Lauren was boasting as Dr. Saville escorted her out. "I won several most-beautiful-baby contests, you know."

Rebecca aimed a covert glance at her employer.

As usual he was fully attentive to his patient, even though Lauren's egocentric jabbering and constant fishing for compliments could vex a saint. Lois was right, she decided. He does look a bit bedraggled this morning. Or as Rebecca used to mispronounce the word for years: bed-aggled. His normally neat hair was slightly tousled, as if he'd just run his hand through it and not bothered with the comb. Also, there was a heaviness to his eyelids, a rather sexy heaviness that drew Rebecca in at first glance.

She couldn't get the thought out of her head that that was how Dr. John Saville would look in the morning after a long night of lovemaking. That was how his lover would see him when she first opened her eyes, the tousled dark hair, the sleep-heavy gaze, and then his mouth that would...

She startled herself out of the reverie. Going down that road was insane, and she would not do it. Never. Absolutely never.

Worried, she knelt down to count bottles of medicine stored on a low shelf.

Preoccupied, she didn't hear Lauren leave, nor did she realize John Saville stood in the doorway watching her.

For a moment, seeing her, he completely forgot what he meant to say. Rebecca's cotton velour skirt had slid up high on her thighs when she knelt. She had gorgeous legs, well formed and nicely muscled. And at this angle her V-neck blouse gave him a tantalizing view of her breasts.

Abruptly he became aroused by the unexpected sight. And just his luck, she chose that same moment to glance up and catch him ogling her.

Way to go, Saville, he berated himself. You give the woman stern lectures on professionalism, now here you stand before her with a tent in your trousers.

It brought back all the memories of being called to the blackboard in high school right in the middle of erotic fantasies.

He lowered the patient chart in his hand, hoping she didn't notice what he was hiding.

Rebecca quickly stood up, smoothing her skirt.

"Is there something you need, Doctor?" she inquired.

The irony of her words made him feel like a thief caught in the act. This woman was wonderful with the patients, he thought. She was confident, intelligent and warm. With him, however, she always had a cold manner. Her frostiness toward him belied the red in her hair and the pearly allure of her complexion.

"Yes, Doctor?" she repeated, and her haughty tone plus his consternation at being caught scoping her out made him defensive.

"I just wanted to say," he practically barked at her, "that I accept the apology you tried to make on Friday night."

He had intended to be more gracious about it. Now his good intentions backfired. He watched red splotches of anger leap into her cheeks.

"Well, thank you very much," she replied coldly. "It's so nice to be forgiven."

The deep, frowning crease was back between his eyebrows. "Fine," he snapped back, his insides churning like molten metal.

He disappeared, and moments later his office door shut with a resounding slam.

Lois now ventured back from the front of the office. She looked in at Rebecca, who was still flushed with anger, and shook her head.

"You two are going at it already?" she asked her friend.

Rebecca fumed. "There are other jobs, you know."

"Simmer down, hon," Lois soothed. "That vein over your temple looks like a hyperventillating worm."

"I can't help it, Lo. He gets me so agitated."

A faint smile lifted one corner of Lois's mouth.

"Yes," she agreed with a knowing little glimmer in her eyes. "He certainly does, doesn't he?"

Rebecca's eyebrows arched in surprise when, toward the middle of the afternoon, Hazel arrived unannounced requesting a drop-by appointment with Dr. Saville.

"You were just here last week," she reminded the older woman.

"Honey, I'm not *quite* senile yet. I know that."

"What's the problem?"

Hazel poked a hand inside her big raffia tote and produced a brown bottle. "It's these new vitamins I want to try," she explained. "Mitty Ames swears by them. I want the doctor to look at the label and tell me what he thinks."

"Hazel," Rebecca said suspiciously, "you're practically

an expert on vitamins. Dr. Winthrop used to send patients to *you* for advice.''

''Well, my lands,'' Hazel complained. ''Is this Russia? I come with a simple request, and I get the third degree. Is a drop-by a problem? If he's too busy…''

''No,'' Rebecca assured her, eyes cutting to the monthly appointment planner on Lois's desk. ''I think he'll see you, Hazel. He'll be finishing up with a patient in a few minutes, and there's no one else scheduled today because he has to go to the hospital later for two surgeries. I'll ask him.''

''Thank you, sweet love,'' Hazel replied, unperturbed by Rebecca's searching gaze.

Five minutes later Hazel and John Saville were once again alone in the examination room.

''Well, young lady,'' he said, his eyes nearly as curious as Rebecca's had been, ''what's this about vitami—''

''Oh, never mind the vitamins,'' she said impatiently. ''That was just a fib to get me past Rebecca. What is it you youngsters require nowadays—an electric cattle prod?''

He blinked as if she had spoken in Chinese. ''Excuse me?''

''Oh, excuse a cat's tail, you hunka-hunka burning love. Just tell me straight up—John, are you attracted to Rebecca O'Reilly?''

He actually gaped in astonishment, unused to having his authority ripped right out from under him. ''I, uh…that is…''

''Just spit it out,'' she urged him. ''Yes or no?''

He scrubbed his face with his hands and slacked into the chair beside her.

''I'll take that as a definite, unequivocal yes,'' she told him.

He watched her, his handsome face a study in cloaking his emotions.

"So what are you waiting for, an embossed invitation?"

He smiled a bitter smile. "If you're thinking that Miss O'Reilly and I might hit it off one day, you can forget it. For starters," he assured her, "she despises me down deep in her bones. Hell if I know why."

"She's had her heart broken by your kind."

He snorted. "What do you mean, by my kind? I may not have grown up in Mystery, but let me assure all of the townsfolk, I am the exact same species you are."

Hazel shook her head at the folly of this younger generation. "You just remind her of the wounds she's had to lick. That's all."

"We've all been wounded, one way or another. I can't make her heal," he stated in a monotone. His dismissal was to Hazel like blood to a hound.

"Maybe she's not the one to heal," Hazel said, her eyes narrowing. "Maybe it's the doctor who must heal thyself."

He ran his hands through his hair in exasperation. The Matriarch of Mystery was way too close to the truth. Rebecca was out of his scope. She was too unpredictable and dismissive for him to approach her. The shallow socialites he'd been involved with in the past few years were just his type. Mercenary. He knew all about that. Too many beatings from a bitter father obsessed with never failing had taught him nothing about love but more than he needed to know about mercenaries.

"Young man, I'll tell you no lies," Hazel said quietly. "What you see now as obstacles are really only speed bumps on the road to true love. You and Rebecca are a perfect couple."

"Perfect couple? Frankly, Hazel, that's a little over the top for me. I can't even begin to fathom her mind, what she—"

Hazel waved his speech aside as if she were shooing a fly. "That's all your college and medical training confusing you. Don't waste time analyzing Rebecca. Trying to figure out a woman's mind is like trying to figure out what came before once-upon-a-time. Accept what she is and enjoy it. She's an amazing creature.''

He greeted this with a long, fluming sigh. ''I don't dispute you there. It's just…I mean, I don't…''

''I know what the problem is,'' Hazel insisted, ''you look at her and see all that red in her hair and you think, Fire. All red blazing fire. But deep inside, you believe there's nothing but ice inside you. She's so different from you that you can't even imagine the two of you ever getting along. Erotic fantasies, sure, but you can't imagine actually coexisting outside of bed. Am I right?''

He said nothing, damning himself with silence.

''I'm used to being right,'' she said shamelessly. ''You just take it from an old rancher and equestrian. Love is no different from learning to ride a horse. First you walk, then you trot, then you lope, then you canter, and *then* you gallop. One step at a time, and before you know it, you're *there*.''

Hazel rose.

John rose, too, watching her with a look of baffled amazement. She had cut to the deepest matters of his heart with the same surgical speed and precision he prided himself on.

''Hang in there like the man I know you are, and she'll crater,'' Hazel insisted, using an old miner's term for caving in. ''And don't ever worry about a woman being too 'different' from you. That's why we're called the opposite sex, get it?''

He saw that she had pulled her checkbook out, and he waved it aside. ''Put that back in your purse. If anything, you should send *me* the bill for today's visit.''

Hazel grinned. ''No, I'll pay. You want Rebecca to think we're conspiring against her? You *will* have troubles then.

Tell you what. Just give me a long ride in that beautiful car of yours sometime, and we'll call it even.''

"Deal," he agreed.

"Hang in there," she repeated. "And good luck. You know, Rebecca's a little like a fine sports car herself. She's temperamental and a little complicated. But, mister, once you get her purring, I'll bet you're in for the ride of your life.''

Six

Rebecca's interaction with her employer in the supply room left her in a foul mood for much of the day. At first, catching him staring at her had been flattering—even a little bit of a turn-on. But then it had all blown to kingdom come with their chilly exchange of words.

Hazel's frustrating secrecy hadn't helped her mood any, either. As the disastrous date with Rick Collins proved, Hazel's good intentions could become a major pain. Rebecca still suspected Hazel was behind the strange events of the date with Rick. No way could Hazel ever have believed she and Rick would get along. Too, Hazel's cowboys were intensely loyal, and it would have been simple for one of them to have deflated Rick's tire in the parking lot.

And evidently the canny old matchmaker hadn't emptied her bag of tricks just yet.

The splendid spring day waiting for her outside after work was a tonic to Rebecca's mood. The short drive from

Mystery to her apartment near Valley General took her across some of the prettiest country in the valley. The area's magnificent silver spruces were swollen with new sap and budding into leaf, the meadows and pastures dotted with bright-red Indian paintbrush.

At one point she passed the outlying pastures of the Lazy M. She backed her foot off the gas pedal, slowing down to watch a six-year-old sorrel stud Hazel had named King Solomon.

Drunk on spring sunshine, the stallion raced along beside her in the huge pasture. His muscular quarters gleamed with the power and length of his stride; the breathtaking speed increased as the bunched muscles contracted and released like tightly wound springs exploding, thrusting and again thrusting, powerful and forceful....

Again she saw John Saville athletically leaping out of his roadster, again she felt his hand brushing her calf with charged force....

Rebecca realized she was breathing more quickly, her heart thumping loudly in her ears.

"Girl," she muttered out loud, "forget about that disaster with Rick Collins. You *do* need another date."

There was a certain growing priority that she needed to take care of, and that wasn't about to happen without an eligible guy. Not necessarily Mr. Right. Maybe Mr. Right-Now would do.

Feeling like a confirmed old maid already, Rebecca passed an uneventful evening reading and then watching an old Bogart movie on cable until bedtime. Not too long after she opened out the studio couch into her bed and fell asleep, the telephone on the end table startled her awake.

"Huh?" was all she could manage when she first answered the phone, speaking through clinging cobwebs of sleep. The ruby-red numerals on the digital clock showed it was just past 2:00 a.m.

"Becky, hon, wake up, it's Lois. There's been a terrible accident."

Lois's words had the force of cold water in the face.

Rebecca shot up to a sitting position, suddenly wide awake.

An accident. She thought instantly of her father, who spent most of his life driving. The consummate travelling salesman. Then logic assured her that that news would not be coming from Lois. No sooner did the fear pass, however, when another possibility seemed to make her blood turn in her veins: Hazel.

"Do you have any idea," Lois pressed on before she could ask her anything, "where Dr. Saville might be?"

"Isn't he at home? But how would I—Lois, what happened?"

"Oh, Becky, it sounds just awful. A crowded bus lost its brakes on the interstate. It overturned on the western slope of Copper Mountain and went over the embankment."

"Copper Mountain." Ice encased Rebecca's spine. "Lois, that stretch is almost all cliffs, not just an embankment."

"We've been monitoring it at home on Merrill's policeband radio. It's pure chaos right now, Becky. There are several fatalities and a whole lot of serious injuries. Trouble is it's impossible to get to the seriously wounded until a special evacuation team with the right equipment can arrive from Fort Mackenzie."

Rebecca, trapping the cordless phone between her ear and her shoulder to free her hands, was already hurriedly stepping into a pair of jeans.

"State troopers have been able to lower two doctors and a nurse from Lutheran Hospital down on ropes," Lois continued. "They've set up a triage, but they still desperately need surgeons to do emergency intervention for a few of the badly injured who can't hold out much longer. Just to stop internal bleeding until they can get them out of there."

"Oh, my God," Rebecca breathed as the real shock of it started to settle in. Lois was talking about the most difficult kind of medical care imaginable—surgery at the trauma scene itself. But this was Mystery Valley, a quiet, uneventful place where little besides routine accidents ever stressed the medical community. They simply weren't ready for this.

"I've tried Dr. Saville's house and the office," Lois lamented. "Repeatedly. But it's no use. I get the message machine both places. It just doesn't make sense. I mean, he's not exactly a party animal—not during the week, anyway. Besides, he had back-to-back surgeries this afternoon. He should've gone home tired long ago."

"Yeah, that's right, he had surgery," Rebecca chimed in, moving the phone so she could tug on a warm pullover. "I know where he might be. One morning when I was early at work, I found him asleep on that big couch in his office. He told me he sleeps there sometimes when he's working late on his journal articles or tired after surgery. It's lots closer than going out to his place."

"That makes sense, all right, especially with the phone on his desk," Lois added. "It only rings on low volume, remember? Loud ringing always startled Dr. Winthrop, he had that crazy theory that every startle reflex takes one day off the heart. So he set it on low volume, then broke the selector off."

"Sure, we both teased him about it. Well, keep dialing the number," Rebecca implored her. "I'll drive to the office right now. If he's not there, I'm going to the accident scene on my own. They may need more nurses."

"Last I heard, they do. You be careful, babe, and good luck. I'll keep trying the office."

The old Bronco was no speed demon, but with the night-time roads empty, Rebecca floored it. She made it to the clinic in Mystery in less than ten minutes.

"Thank God," she murmured aloud as she wheeled into the asphalt parking lot, and the headlights revealed the doctor's long, low-slung Alfa Romeo parked close to the building.

She unlocked the glass double doors and slapped at the master light switch, filling the entire suite with soft, indirect lighting. Even as she raced back toward the private office at the end of the hall, she heard the low, insistent chirring of his phone as Lois dialed.

She flung open his door and saw a supine form stretched out on the couch even before she switched on the lights.

"Dr. Saville! Doctor, wake up!"

In the few seconds before he responded, she got a strong impression of the slumbering man. A gray exhaustion was evident in the handsome face, the cumulative toll of his secret weekend plus a grueling session in surgery.

Despite her urgency, however, she couldn't help appreciating the fact that his shirt was off. His pectorals were hard and sloping, his abs and lats like taut steel bands. A fine mat of dark hair formed a silky vee on his chest. His stomach was flat and hard, and for a moment she couldn't help wishing he'd taken his trousers off, too.

"What?" he demanded, sitting up quickly. "What's wrong?"

First she picked up the ringing phone and told Lois she'd found him. Then she quickly filled him in on the emergency.

He took it in stride with his usual calm efficiency, already collecting extra surgical instruments and supplies for his leather jump kit even before she finished speaking.

"Get plenty of sterile gauze, sponges and alcohol wipes," he instructed her. "Bring clamps and silk sutures and number-three catgut for closing up. It doesn't have to be fancy work up there, it just has to hold until we can get them stabilized in a hospital. Looks like you'll be doing some sewing tonight, Becky."

Becky.

It startled her, coming from his lips.

"The big problem," he worried aloud, "will be anesthetic. I can do locals, but that won't be enough. I wish we had a general anesthetic to put them under."

"I was taught the emergency procedures for administering chloroform with a pad," she told him. "We have a few bottles."

"Sure, that'll help. It's a little crude and risky, but better than nothing if the choice is life or death."

As they let themselves out into the nighttime chill, he asked her if she knew the way to the accident scene.

She nodded.

"My car is pretty quick," he worried out loud, "but I'm almost out of gas and there's no place to fill up close by."

"I'll drive. My Bronco's probably more useful up there, anyway. It's got four-wheel drive."

"How far away are we talking?"

"Twenty minutes north on Route 23."

"If those victims are lucky—" he hoped out loud as they climbed into the Bronco "—they'll be airlifted before we even get there."

Up on the slope of Copper Mountain, luck was in short supply. A dozen or more emergency vehicles, lights winking eerily, had assembled just off the shoulder of a sharp, nearly vertical embankment. The new arrivals learned that the military-rescue team from Fort Mackenzie was still en route. A mix-up had caused the request to be delayed.

"We just now managed to lower a couple of paramedics down there," a state trooper explained. "That's helped some. But neither one of the guys down there is a surgeon, and they're at wit's end. They'll be mighty glad to see you, Doc."

Even in the lurid glow of the police vehicle lights Rebecca could see how tired John Saville looked. Far below, flares and a few smaller lights marked the accident scene.

"This rig looks pretty roomy," John told the cop, meaning the doughnut harness the trooper was buckling around him. "Will it hold two people?"

The trooper nodded. "It's designed to hold up to three, actually."

The doctor looked at Rebecca.

"Then lower both of us at one time," he suggested. "You said it takes five minutes to descend. I can't get to work without my assist nurse, and we've already wasted enough time."

It's a purely practical arrangement, Rebecca reminded herself as she snuggled up close to her employer. He stood behind her, arms encircling her, as the harness was buckled.

"Keep still," the trooper called out as they were lowered over the berm of the drop-off. "You don't want to start twirling—keep the embankment in front of you. Any problem, just give us a holler."

At first her nervous jitters kept Rebecca from thinking about how intimately close they were—so close she could feel every muscular contour of his body pressing against her. But the going was easier than she'd expected—in part because he did most of the work to keep them balanced, and the cops up above were handling the weight of descent.

"Piece of cake," he assured her, lips so close to her ear

she could feel the warmth of his breath. "I'm a rock climber from way back."

His words jolted her memory of what Hazel had told her. It was during a rock-climbing vacation that he supposedly met Louise Wallant.

She chastised herself when she felt a little inner spasm of jealousy—here she was, being lowered down a mountain in the middle of the night, with people hurt and dying below, yet she had time to feel jealousy for a man who saw her as a social inferior.

All that, however, could not prevent her from physically reacting to his nearness. The hand not clutching his jump kit kept brushing her breasts, unintended caresses that nonetheless triggered tickles of desire—especially since, in her hurry to find him tonight, she hadn't worn a bra. And each time they dropped farther down, gravity made her surge against him. Before long it was obvious he was aroused.

Moments later they reached the scene below, and Rebecca felt her heart sink when she saw the badly mangled and crumpled bus lying on one side, its progress finally stopped by a line of trees. Everywhere she looked, troopers were holding flashlights while various members of the medical team worked over the injured. Almost the only sounds were occasional pitiful groans and the stacatto crackling of radio static.

Dan Woodyard, a pediatrician Rebecca knew slightly from her days at Valley General, took a quick break to help them out of their harness and fill them in.

"Thank God for you two," he greeted them. "We've treated most of the visible trauma wounds. But there are several with internal bleeding—severed arteries and, in one case, I think a ruptured spleen. Hell, the only surgeries I do are tonsils. All we've been able to do is give them clotting factor and treat them for shock."

Woodyard sounded close to losing it. Even medical

school, Rebecca realized sympathetically, couldn't harden him for something like this.

John gripped one of his shoulders and gave it a reassuring squeeze.

"You've done great, Dan," he assured his colleague in a firm, calming tone. "Who's the other doctor, and what's his specialty?"

"Jim Routan from Lutheran. He's a semiretired G.P. with little surgical experience, mostly does screening physicals. He's over on the other side of the bus with the burn victims and spinal traumas."

While this report was forthcoming, Dr. Woodyard led John and Rebecca to a group of four patients lying under blankets.

"They've been sedated," Dan reported. "The elderly woman on the right is the possible ruptured spleen."

While Rebecca checked each patient's vital signs, John made a quick check of each victim's injuries to set his priority of treatment. She had already noticed something— his arrival on the scene, his calm, confident competence, had created a sense of purpose and control. Dan and the others seemed to settle down, inspired by John's unflappable manner under duress.

"We're not really operating, this is surgical intervention to control their bleeding," John reminded her in a low tone. "They require complicated repairs and a team of surgeons. All we can do now, though, is just open them quick and place clips on any severed arteries, pack them with sponges and close them with wide stitches and pressure dressings. This isn't even E.R. stuff, it's basically battlefield first aid. You okay?"

She expected fear to show in her voice, but she spoke up firmly. "I'm fine."

"Just hang in there and don't let anything get to you. Got your chloroform ready?"

Feeling like a beleaguered Civil War nurse, Rebecca soaked a gauze pad and carefully administered a general anesthetic to the first patient. She concentrated on counting out the seconds accurately, removing and then again applying the pad, while John worked.

She was not normally a surgical nurse, and the sights before her became even more stark in the glare of the flashlight being held by an ashen-faced trooper.

But the need to stay strong for these tragic victims kept her steady, focused and alert. So, too, did John Saville's steady hand and manner. She steeled her nerves, and after each patient's internal bleeding was controlled, Rebecca closed with deliberately wide stitches and dressed each wound, while John administered a local to the next patient.

"What's the word on that evacuation team?" John asked the cop as they were finishing the last patient. "I'm not too impressed by their response time."

"Let me check," the trooper holding their light offered. "Last I heard, they had some delay locating their chopper pilot."

He spoke into his radio handset, then listened for a minute. "Choppers are just now passing over Disappearing Lake, Doc," he reported. "Still another twenty-five minutes. Fort Mackenzie is practically on the Canadian border."

Dan Woodyard had joined them again. "Think she'll make it?" he asked, meaning the elderly woman with the possibly ruptured spleen.

"Her pulse is fluttery and her breathing rapid and shallow," Rebecca reported. "Systolic blood pressure is fluctuating between eighty and ninety."

"My God," Dan muttered, "she's barely pumping blood."

"I think she may have a preexisting heart problem," John added tersely. "Going into third-stage shock has taxed it to the limit. We could lose her at any moment. There are ambulances topside—how quickly could they get her to Lutheran?''

"Less than ten minutes," Dan replied. "And the E.R. is prepped and waiting. I even got their blood types called in.''

"That settles it, then. At best, it'll be well over a half hour before that rescue team can extract her and get her into surgery. If I take her up now, we can have her under the scalpel in maybe half that time.''

"Man, that's one rough climb going up," Dan said, his voice heavy with doubt.

"Don't I know it? And it might well kill her. But do you agree she probably won't last a half hour?''

"I do," Dan affirmed. "I haven't watched many people expire, but she sure seems close. She's practically without blood pressure.''

"How 'bout you, Becky?" John inquired, turning to her. "Think we should move her now or wait?''

It startled her that he was actually turning to her for help in this decision.

"If you both believe she may well die, anyway, then isn't it better to take some action? Judging from her vital signs, I vote for taking her up.''

"That's the girl," he approved. "No waffling.''

While the trooper notified the officers up above, Rebecca and Dan helped John into the harness rig. All three of them carefully lifted the unconscious woman until John had her in a fireman's carry.

"You two come up behind us as a safety net," he instructed Rebecca and Dan. "One on each side of me. Be ready in case she starts to slip from my grasp.''

When the other two rescuers were buckled into safety harnesses, the trooper gave the signal and they started up the steep slope. Although the men above were doing most of the pulling, John still had a grueling struggle supporting the injured woman. Rebecca saw him straining up ahead of her, his breathing growing deeper and more labored.

But his superb physical condition saw him through it. They got the injured woman above and into an ambulance in amazingly quick time. They returned below to help with the rest. By the time the rescue team from Fort Mackenzie arrived to medivac the rest, the elderly woman was already undergoing surgery.

"She's critical but stable," reported a jubilant Dan, who was in touch with the hospital on his cell phone. "Looks like you didn't make that climb for nothing, John. Early word is she's going to make it."

"Question is, will I?" John groused as he and Rebecca trudged toward her Bronco.

It was nearly 6:00 a.m. Rebecca felt weary and physically depleted and knew he must feel even worse.

But she also felt an inner swelling of new admiration for this man she *thought* she had already neatly pegged as conceited and coldhearted. Even half-dead with exhaustion, he rose to an incredible challenge. His quiet, calm, unassuming leadership had steadied the rest of them. He had been selfless to a fault, and suddenly she wanted very much to make sure *he* was fussed over a little, too. He certainly deserved it.

"You need some sleep," she told him. "Why don't I just take you straight to your place? Lois can call your morning appointments and cancel. Then one of us can come pick you up later."

He mulled this over, then shook his head as Rebecca performed a U-turn, heading back toward Mystery. "Actually, I don't feel all that tired. Besides, I hate it to no end when doctors cancel out on patients. Anyway, as I recall, my last appointment is at noon. It's better if I just tough it out and stay awake, then go to bed this afternoon. Assuming, that is, that my nurse can make it, too?''

She smiled at him. ''I'm not really tired, either. Nothing a quick shower can't fix.''

He returned her smile with a grateful one of his own. ''Two workaholics strike a bargain. Just take me back to my car, and I'll find someplace to have breakfast and coffee.''

''Nothing's open right now,'' she reminded him. ''This is Mystery, remember? If you insist on staying awake, why not come on back to my place? I'll fix us some breakfast, then give you a ride to your car so you can go home and shower and change.''

''Breakfast—and at least a gallon of black coffee?''

''Cowboy coffee,'' she promised. ''Strong enough to float a horseshoe.''

They both laughed, enjoying the feel of mirth after their ordeal on the mountain.

''Best offer I've had all night,'' he assured her.

Rebecca watched the newly risen sun flame on the eastern horizon of Mystery Valley, a salmon-pink blush. Just a day ago she'd been trading insults with John Saville; now she was taking him home for breakfast.

Oh, what a difference a night can make.

Seven

The early-morning sun was bright but the air was still chilly when they arrived at Rebecca's efficiency apartment. She brewed a big pot of coffee. Then, feeling self-conscious in such close quarters, she selected a change of clothing and excused herself for a quick shower. She changed into a seawater-blue knit dress, then started working on a couple of western omelettes.

Although he had no clean change of clothing, John accepted her invitation to shower. He emerged, hair freshly slicked back, just in time to enjoy a well-earned hot breakfast.

"Pardon my 5:00 a.m. shadow," he quipped, rubbing his scratchy, blue-black beard stubble.

"I like it," Rebecca assured him sincerely. "Makes you look like a soap opera hunk."

"Please, lady, no autographs until I've eaten."

They both laughed.

She cast a rueful glance around her little cubbyhole of an apartment, sorry now that she had procrastinated in finding a bigger place. Partly it was a sort of spite that made her keep it, for she suspected the nothing apartment and the lack of good background were the reasons Brian had dumped her.

"You must be feeling claustrophobic," she apologized. "I've been inside your house before you owned it. This entire apartment is about the size of your breakfast nook."

"Yeah, but you know what?" he retorted between forkfuls of steaming omelette. "My place is about as homey as a post office lobby. Your place is cozy. And even two showers in a row didn't use up all the hot water. I'm lucky to finish one at my house. Seriously, it must have a one-gallon water heater."

He didn't say all this to be patronizing or merely polite, she realized, but seemed sincere. Ever since her crushing experience with Brian, she had possessed an invisible antenna for detecting snobbery and rejection. But she spotted none in John's manner with her now.

As she topped up his coffee, he nodded toward a framed photo on the television set.

"Nice-looking couple. Especially the woman. From the way you favor her, I'm guessing it's your mom and dad?"

She nodded. "My mother died of a brain tumor when I was in junior high."

"I'm sorry to hear it," he told her with sincere feeling. "She was taken so young, it must've been tough on you."

"I don't know what I would've done without Hazel. My dad's on the road a lot, especially since Mom passed away. Hazel practically adopted me after her death."

Realization sparked in his eyes. "So that's why she takes such an interest in you."

"What do you mean?" she asked cautiously.

He seemed to realize, however, that he'd misspoken. Instead of answering, admitting that he and Hazel had been discussing her, he diplomatically changed topics. "You said your dad's on the road a lot. Is he in sales?"

"Uh-huh. That and consulting. He sells and installs security systems, mostly for small businesses. He works a three-state area."

She didn't add, however, that he had often been unemployed when she was younger, or that his drinking and womanizing had started more than one rumor wave rolling through Mystery Valley.

"How 'bout your father?" she asked. "You already told me he retired from the military. Did he start a second career?"

"Not really," was all he told her, his eyes suddenly grave and evasive.

She'd noticed how he seldom gave any information on his own background, but only elicited it from others. "This omelette," he added quickly, "is the best I've ever had."

"Thanks," she replied, not fooled by his diversionary tactic. He didn't want to talk about himself, and she would respect that. It wasn't the kind of thing two professionals took to work, anyway, and she knew she'd do best to remember it.

She gathered up their plates from the L-shaped counter that served as a kitchen table, rinsed them and set them in the dishwasher. His intensely blue gaze followed her.

"That backless stool can't be too comfortable," she said, mainly to break the awkward silence. "You're welcome to take your coffee into the living room." She glanced apologetically at the fold-out couch that was still a knot of blankets and sheets from last night's frantic dash out the door. "But maybe I should pick up first—"

"Forget about it. Even a messy fold-out looks good after that mountain climb." He paused. "I guess I'm more bushed than I thought. I hardly slept at all this weekend."

He suddenly stopped, again seeming to realize he had inadvertently said too much. His gaze fled from hers, and she chastised herself for feeling another sting of jealousy. There it was again, obvious as an elephant in the living room: his secret weekends.

She reminded herself she had no proof he was trysting with Louise Wallant. Besides, even if he was, what business was it of hers if he kept a woman in every town in the West?

It was none of her business. None of her business at all. They were two professionals who had found camaraderie in a black moment. The breaking of the ice was going to help their office relationship by leaps and bounds, but it was not going to change the facts: he was all over Louise Wallant every other weekend, and Rebecca was not going to take the chance, however small it seemed this morning, that he was another Brian Gage.

Nope. She wasn't even going to take the chance.

John settled back on the couch, his legs stretched out across the mattress. He was less inclined to make conversation since his careless reference to the past weekend. What, he wondered idly, would she think if she knew his sordid background? If she ever got an inkling of where he was going, what he was doing during those regular road trips of his, he would have to explain where he came from. He'd have to explain the trailer by the dump, the awful beatings and the place he found sanctuary, the place he now went to every other weekend in a minuscule attempt to pay back those who'd helped him find his self-respect.

If he could just remember to remain quiet, he wouldn't have to face any questions. Nor have to confess the ugly answers.

He felt his muscles going slack with weariness. Rebecca continued to work in the small kitchenette, as if looking for excuses not to be too close to him. Like right now—she was replacing an empty roll of paper towels.

What, that couldn't wait?

She was avoiding him. He released a dark, ironic smile. He wondered if it was because she sensed how much he'd ached to kiss her tempting, heart-shaped lips ever since they'd got in her car this morning. And that flawless ivory skin of hers, how he wanted to caress her nude body, how he burned at the thought of those slender, perfect legs of hers locked behind his back and her moaning...moaning...

But even as he felt those thoughts arousing him, he warned himself *not* to ruin this hard-won peace between them. Look how long they'd been at each other's throats. Now, as a result of their shared experience at the accident scene, a rare truce had been established.

Just because she's being good to you now, he cautioned himself, doesn't mean she feels what you feel.

How *could* she? They were as different as push and pull. He'd seen how she behaved at work with Lois and the patients: relaxed, fun loving, always kidding around with a smile in her eyes as well as on those eminently kissable, pouty lips of hers.

To her, in contrast, I must seem as interesting as a concrete piling.

Until this moment he hadn't fully realized how much last night's exertions had depleted him. Now the bill was coming due. He was having trouble keeping his thoughts focused and rational. The daydreams were running into the realities. Rebecca was here with him and they were professionals, cool and detached. But he still couldn't stop the pictures of her in his mind with her hair wild and her heart anything but cool and detached.

He set his cup and saucer down on the glass-top coffee table, his head nodding slowly forward as his thoughts began to get all jumbled, like a bunch of radio stations drowning each other out....

"If I take you back to your car now," Rebecca suggested above the quiet hum of the dishwasher, "you'll have time to drive home, change and still make your 9:00 a.m. appointment."

She turned to look at him, expecting his reply. Instead she saw that John Saville had fallen sound asleep on the studio couch, half sitting, half lying down.

"John?" she called to him. His first name still felt odd on her lips, but she could hardly be formal under the circumstances.

"John?" she called again, a little louder, still with no results.

"We already know you're a sound sleeper," she told him with a little twinge of regret as she moved closer to wake him.

Her hand inches from his shoulder, she paused, reluctant to wake the poor guy. His breathing was slow and even, his face relaxed and handsome in sleep although his head was crooked awkwardly to one side.

Feeling the guilty pleasure of a voyeur, she studied his face, the fine, straight, patrician nose, the well-defined cheekbones, the strong, broad brow and firm but expressive mouth.

Yes, he was a specimen, all right, no kidding there. But she had never placed all that much importance on looks in a man.

So why, she demanded of herself, are you so in danger of falling in love with him?

At best, he was an enigma to her, keeping to himself, seldom mingling with Mystery's natives except when one of them needed a hernia fixed or their gall bladder out, as

Hazel had. His stiff, unyielding manner was difficult for the more earthy, convivial folks of Mystery to warm up to.

Except now, another part of her pointed out, you've seen past that screen of formality and found a warm, relaxed, humorous person behind it.

Again she thought about their descent together on Copper Mountain, how it had secretly thrilled her to feel his arousal, the physical power and proof of his desire. It was only sexual desire, of course, and she knew men well enough to know that was no rare compliment from a man.

Yet she had no willpower to prevent her from wondering what it would be like to have him as a lover. Nor could she censor the torrid images that made her pulse race.

On top of all that, she did not have the heart to wake him up.

Exhaustion was starting to claim her, too, and he'd done far more physical exertion carrying that injured woman up to the road.

Deciding to take the responsibility on herself, she left a message for Lois on the office machine. She told her they had both put in a long night and the day's appointments would have to be rescheduled. She was careful to say nothing that hinted they were together.

Gently, so as not to wake him, Rebecca removed his shoes. Then she settled him more comfortably on the fold-out couch with a pillow under his head.

For a few moments she wondered where she should sleep—in the nearby overstuffed chair or on the floor.

This is silly, she decided. We're both fully dressed and exhausted. We aren't really going to bed together, it's a question of simple necessity.

She kicked off her shoes and carefully settled in beside him, making sure to maintain some distance.

But despite her exhaustion, it was hard for her to fall asleep. The deep rhythm of his breathing, the unavoidable warmth of his nearness, wouldn't let her mind rest. She lay for a long time reveling in the scent of him that clung to his clothes. Finally sleep came over her like a deep, long shadow.

And she dreamed only of him.

Despite Rebecca's good intentions, when John's eyes eased open several hours later she lay curled tightly against him, her face only inches from his and beautiful in repose, as sensuous as a subtle painting.

His first concern should have been the time and his professional obligations. But even though a quick glance at his watch told him it was well past noon, he couldn't pry himself away from the sleeping beauty beside him.

Her chestnut hair, unrestrained, formed a silken mane against the pillow.

He breathed deeply of it, reveling in the clean, feminine fragrance. Her mouth formed a natural pout in her sleep, and he lightly brushed her lips with his, tasting her in a stolen kiss.

He didn't expect her lips to part readily for him—or the electric response in his loins as she pressed her body warmth even closer.

Their kiss deepened, and a low moan of pent-up desire rose in both of them as his hands caressed her, igniting fires wherever they touched.

"Is it safe to say you're awake?" he managed to say between quickening breaths. "Or am I taking advantage of a sleeping woman?"

"I'm not asleep," she whispered, her tone imploring him to go further. To give more.

"The office," he managed before he greedily tasted her kiss again.

"Taken care of," she assured him, enthralled by her own welling passions. "I called Lois."

Again a low, encouraging moan arose from her as his hands unbuttoned her dress, his mouth kissing her and tasting the exposed skin. One hand caressed the sweeping dip of her hip, the gently rounded stomach, then moved around behind her to join the other hand in unfastening her bra. She felt a luscious, hot pleasure stiffen her nipples as he took each into his mouth, firing her to a dizzy, pulsing ecstasy.

By now her need matched his. The caution that normally controlled her seemed melted like the liquid between her thighs. Instinct and pure rich desire took control now.

Her fingers trembling with desire, she unbuttoned his shirt. She pulled it off, running her hands over his tautly muscled chest. He groaned with the pleasure of contact when he dragged her naked, aroused breasts against him, merging their flesh.

One hand slid under the elastic waistband of her panties to feel the wet warmth of her.

He groaned, as if her arousal was almost painful to him. "It's been too long," he whispered, sliding the panties right off her. He stroked her high on the inside of her thighs, and she opened them wider for him, guiding his fingers with every stroke.

She shuddered, a throaty moan escaping her, when his fingers gently parted the delicate folds of her sex like petals, driving her with quick intensity to a climax. The speed of it shocked her and only made her greedy for more.

"I want you inside me," she begged, fumbling to unbuckle and lower his trousers.

"I want me inside you, too," he assured her, gazing deep into her eyes. "But one of us has to be responsible. I don't have any protection. How 'bout you?"

"Believe it or not," she confessed, "until this moment that's never been an issue with me—almost, a few times, but not quite."

He stared down at her as if not quite believing.

She controlled her reeling thoughts long enough to per suade him. All she knew now was want and the fiery drive to appease it. John Saville was another woman's lover and would probably never be hers again, but time was standing still for once. All the instincts that saved her from Brian had abandoned her. She only knew that while her mind told her it was long-suppressed carnal greed driving her, her heart had her fooled that it was love. She wanted John Saville, wanted him now, because all the lies had lined up just right, and she was blinded and, oh, so hungry.

"This should be the absolute safest time for me," she whispered, pulling him onto her. "That's as responsible as Nurse Becky can be right now, Doctor."

He closed his eyes as if the emotions inside him roiled in conflict. Finally, as if damned, he settled himself be tween her thighs. "Don't be nervous," he soothed as he entered her. "It's going to be nice, you'll see."

Mixed in with the breathless heat of her desire was a little fear of the unknown, but he'd told her the truth. For just a brief moment, as he opened her tight resistance, she was uncomfortable. But he was gentle, and the slight pain immediately gave way to massive wellings of pleasure that made her whisper for more.

His gentleness, in turn, gave way to an insistent mas culine hunger that made his hips move faster and faster plunge harder and harder. Again, yet again, she rose on fast waves of sexual climax, each one stronger and more sat isfying than the one preceding it.

Finally, just when she was sure the intensity of her re sponses must make her pass out, he exploded inside her taking her up with him one last time in a mutual peak of ecstatic pleasure.

Once again exhausted, though this time by pleasure, he drifted off to sleep. Her last coherent picture was a dazed tangle of arms and legs before she joined him in slumber.

Eight

John's eyes slowly focused on his watch: 3:15 p.m.

"We've been zoned out for hours," he marveled.

Still curled up beside him, Rebecca knew she was awake by her sudden self-consciousness about her nudity. She pulled the sheet up to hide her exposed breasts, but she made no effort to dress because that would mean leaving his side and killing the moment.

Sick in her heart, she came to the desperate realization that she was heading for a fall. She might rationalize that she had taken John Saville to her bed as a Mr. Right-Now, but deep down she knew he meant more. Much more. And she had no right to him. What they'd done was wrong, without commitment, and there had been none. They'd let the moment take them by the throat, and now he would have to leave, and she would have to pretend the most earth-shattering joy she'd ever known had never happened.

"Maybe I shouldn't ask," he said, lips brushing her ear, "but was your first time worth the wait?"

"Mmm," she replied with a mysterious, hurt little smile "Remember, Doctor, I have nothing to compare it with."

"That disappointing, huh?"

"Well, if you must know, I...I really have no complaints to register." Even to her the words sounded forced and distant, but she was too afraid to relinquish her cover and blurt out the truth of what she felt.

She glanced down. "Only a tiny bit of blood, too. Is that usual?"

"Concerning the deflowering of virgins," he assured her. "I can only quote my worthy nurse—I have nothing to compare it with."

"So it was a first for both of us, huh?" Her lips, swollen from the passion of their kisses, tilted in another little smile

He kissed them, and she suddenly felt another stirring of desire. Yet at the back of her mind the seeds of doubt had already been planted.

The passion of their lovemaking had been deep and un-deniable, but, she reminded herself, it was almost acciden-tal. They had bonded during a terrible emergency, then got-ten mutually turned on by unintended physical contact during sleep.

Sure, the secret truth was that she had probably fallen for him, and she was ready and eager to keep right on going. But caution was back in terrible force. Now, more than anything, she wanted to retain her pride. She had to be coldly rational and not let him or the experience with him make her fall. Their joining had been a heat-of-the-moment thing, no more. Tomorrow she had to show up for work and allow him the same benefit without being clingy and needful.

They were not in love, she told herself. Hell, they hadn' even been on a date. She had to keep things cool so she could continue with her job. So she wouldn't get hurt.

She looked at him, desperately wanting to be glib. Instead, his appearance made her smile.

"What are you grinning about now?" he demanded.

"A word I used to mispronounce—bedraggled. I used to say 'bed-raggled' instead of bedraggled. But bed-raggled is exactly how we look now."

He touched the wild, tangled mane of her hair. She noticed even his short coal-black hair was so mussed the part had disappeared.

Almost grimly, he looked over her shoulder and heaved a sigh. "The light's blinking like crazy on your answering machine," he said with resignation. "I didn't even hear the phone ringing. I guess it's turned off."

"Nope," she blurted out.

They both looked at each other in amazement.

"I guess we were tired," she offered.

Unwilling to speak her thoughts out loud, she wished she could immerse herself in their lovemaking until everything mundane and ordinary was washed away again.

But that wasn't the real world. And the real world was intruding with each passing second, and with each flashing light on her machine.

"Maybe you'd better check it," he suggested. "They might be looking for me."

She wanted desperately to ask him if it would shame him to be found asleep in her small apartment, but she didn't want to ruin the moment with a truthful answer. Memories of Brian assailed her. She knew she had to manage this incident so it turned out differently, but the only route seemed to be to detach, to assiduously remain uninvolved and without expectation.

That meant she couldn't let herself fall into bed with him again. Lovemaking was only going to lead to confession and ultimately rejection. She didn't want the messiness of it. Her heart was tattered enough.

Stoically she left the bed and quickly began to dress.

He lay back and watched her, sensing the change in h[e]
manner.

Standing, he slipped on his trousers as she crossed to th[e]
answering machine and poked the play button.

"Becky, hon," boomed an overly jovial male voic[e]
"it's Dad. I'm calling from my hotel room in Greeley, Co[l]
orado. I just saw your picture on the news. Congratulation[s]
I'm really proud of you, kiddo. I should be coming by [to]
see you in a couple of weeks, assuming you aren't to[o]
famous to squeeze the old man in. Later, hon."

John stared at her as the message clicked off, his fac[e]
blank with surprise.

"Saw your picture on the news?" he repeated. "Did yo[u]
notice any reporters up there on Copper Mountain?"

"I spotted a van that said Action Four News on th[e]
side," she told him. "That's a station out of Helena. But [I]
didn't notice any cameraman. Of course, I wasn't reall[y]
looking."

She played the next two messages. Similar congratula[-]
tions from Lois and Hazel, plus an assurance from Lo[is]
that she had taken care of rescheduling patients and woul[d]
be holding down the fort.

By now John, too, had dressed. "Guess I should pick u[p]
my car before birds nest in it," he suggested.

She wondered if he was anxious to be gone. She assume[d]
he was. To her, her whole life had changed; as for him, h[e]
was probably ready to get the day rolling after a one-nig[ht]
stand.

Forcing herself to be practical, she went to get the ca[r]
keys. On the outside, she was calm and easygoing; insid[e]
she was roiling with anxiety.

She had never given her virginity to anyone. Now sh[e]
had to accept that her night with him was just a meaningles[s]
tryst. It had come out of the adrenaline and exhaustion o[f]

e accident the night before, and it would dissipate as soon
s they stepped out the door into the daylight.

She might fall in love with him, but he might not want
nurse with a cramped apartment and no status. And she
ad to accept that, as she had accepted Brian's rejection.

"I'm ready to drive you to the office," she replied, more
oolly than she wanted to.

He stared at her.

When he kissed her one last time before they went out-
de, she thought she felt him holding back a little.

And it was only appropriate behavior, she told herself.
hey needed to cool out and be practical. Nothing had
hanged. He was still destined to see Louise Wallant his
ext weekend away, and she was still a single girl.

Nothing had changed.

Yet in her heart she feared everything had changed.

From the sublime to the awkward is but a step, Rebecca
mented as she drove John back to town.

Outwardly she was calm and at peace, even glowing. But
wardly she alternated between sadness and bewilderment
s she grappled with what they had just done and what it
eant.

It wasn't that he'd turned into a beast or anything blatant
ke that. But then she had felt her heart sink like a stone
hen he mentioned her answering machine. When the
orld intruded, she knew it would end, and the world in-
uded quickly, like the opening of the floodgates.

A tumult of silent misery swept through her. Next to her
n the car, the good doctor was still being affectionate but
rowing distant. Perhaps what they'd done weighed heavily
n him, too. Along with regret.

After all, it was one thing to grab a quickie when the
pportunity was presented, another altogether to let it in-
erfere with one's day.

What was it Hazel had called Louise? A target of op portunity.

And now she had become one, too.

"Lo's still here," she commented as they wheeled int the clinic parking lot, speaking mainly just to break th awkward silence between them. "There's her car."

"Thank God one of us has a work ethic," he quipped

He'd obviously meant it for a joke, but she couldn't eve force a small laugh. She sat with the motor idling, waitin for him to get out and agonizing at the awkwardness of th moment.

His arms began to lift, as if he meant to embrace he But then a shadow seemed to cross his face, and he ende up simply bussing her cheek quickly.

"See you tomorrow at work?" he asked, the casualnes of his remark crushing her.

She could only nod. Tears were already stinging her eye and throat. But as she pulled out of the lot, she resolutel defeated her self-pity.

She had often wondered what it would be like when sh finally "did the deed." And she was never exactly sure ju what she expected to feel when it was over or what sh expected to happen. Certainly not something as ol fashioned as a proposal or a promise of eternal love; the again, neither had she expected this odd letdown, as if she simply had her ears pierced and nothing more.

"You fool," she muttered, her eyes flicking to the rea view mirror. "You impulsive little fool."

Her biggest mistake was the belief that the bad exper ence with Brian had immunized her against such vulnerab feelings as she felt now. It was just the opposite—the ol wounds had been ripped open all over again, more painf than ever.

Her other mistake was to believe she could manage all. Blind to her true vulnerability, she had played a stupi

How to validate your
Editor's FREE GIFT "Thank You"

1. Peel off gift seal from front cover. Place it in space provided at right. This automatically entitles you to receive 2 FREE BOOKS and a fabulous mystery gift.

2. Send back this card and you'll get 2 brand-new Silhouette Desire® novels. These books have a cover price of $3.99 each in the U.S. and $4.50 each in Canada, but they are yours to keep absolutely free.

3. There's no catch. You're under no obligation to buy anything. We charge nothing—ZERO—for your first shipment. And you don't have to make any minimum number of purchases—not even one!

4. The fact is, thousands of readers enjoy receiving their books by mail from the Silhouette Reader Service™. They enjoy the convenience of home delivery...they like getting the best new novels at discount prices BEFORE they're available in stores...and they love their *Heart to Heart* subscriber newsletter featuring author news, horoscopes, recipes, book reviews and much more!

5. We hope that after receiving your free books you'll want to remain a subscriber. But the choice is yours— to continue or cancel, any time at all! So why not take us up on our invitation, with no risk of any kind. You'll be glad you did!

6. Don't forget to detach your FREE BOOKMARK. And remember...just for validating your Editor's Free Gift Offer, we'll send you THREE gifts, *ABSOLUTELY FREE!*

GET A FREE MYSTERY GIFT.

YOURS FREE!

SURPRISE MYSTERY GIFT COULD BE YOURS _FREE_ AS A SPECIAL "THANK YOU" FROM THE EDITORS OF SILHOUETTE

Visit us online at
www.eHarlequin.com

The Editor's "Thank You" Free Gifts Include:

- **Two BRAND-NEW romance novels!**
- **An exciting mystery gift!**

PLACE
FREE GIFT
SEAL
HERE

YES! I have placed my Editor's "Thank You" seal in the space provided above. Please send me 2 free books and a fabulous mystery gift. I understand I am under no obligation to purchase any books, as explained on the back and on the opposite page.

326 SDL DCQE

225 SDL DCP9
(S-D-OS-03/01)

NAME   (PLEASE PRINT CLEARLY)

ADDRESS

APT.#   CITY

STATE/PROV.   ZIP/POSTAL CODE

Thank You!

The Silhouette Reader Service™ — Here's how it works:

game: how close could she get to the fire without being burned? Fool that she was, she'd gotten more than close—she'd leaped headlong right into the inferno.

Despite her resolution against self-pity, a tear welled onto her eyelash, trembled there a moment, then splashed onto her cheek, warm and tickly as it zigzagged down. She swiped it quickly away, determined anew not to start feeling sorry for herself.

"If he thinks I'm going to guilt trip him," she promised her reflection in the mirror, "he can just get over it. I can manage this. I *can*."

She'd learned to expect nothing more from any man than he was willing to give. She hadn't once begged Brian to take her back after he unceremoniously dumped her as a hindrance to his lofty career. And she wasn't about to glom on to John Saville, either. Apparently, the number-one challenge for young and good-looking, self-centered doctors, was to keep gold diggers and small-town nothings from blocking their flight paths.

Well, they didn't have to worry about her. She was happy to stay well out of their way.

It occurred to her that she didn't want to return home right now—not when the sense of his presence was still so strong there. She glanced over her shoulder at the stack of overdue library books on the back seat. Right now any excuse would do.

Rather than return to her apartment and ensure the continued laceration of her heart, she decided to visit the county library. She could return the books and spend some time in the periodicals room. That had long been a refuge when she desperately needed to stop her thoughts for a while. Right now she desired nothing more.

"Rebecca! Yoo-hoo, Rebecca!"

She hesitated halfway up the black granite steps of the

county library, not immediately recognizing the voice that was calling her—nor liking it, either. It was shrill and unpleasant, like a crow squawking.

She turned around and saw a trim, attractive woman in her fifties wearing a navy two-piece pant set. Rebecca's stomach went leaden with dread when she recognized—of all the rotten, ironic luck—Barbara Wallant, Louise's mother.

Politeness made her wait for Barbara to catch up even as Rebecca groaned inwardly at the cruel timing.

"Becky O'Reilly, what brings you to the library in the middle of the afternoon?"

She bit back the temptation to reply sarcastically, *A 1990 Ford Bronco brings me.*

"I thought you were working for John Saville?" Barbara added.

"Hi, Mrs. Wallant. I am, it's just, um, we were called out last night to an accident scene. It kept us pretty late, so today is an unscheduled day off."

Obviously Barbara had not seen the TV news yet or she would already know about the Copper Mountain tragedy. She glanced at the books Rebecca carried.

"Well, it's wonderful, Becky, that you're trying to better yourself."

"They're just mystery novels," she replied dryly, but Barbara gushed on as if not hearing her.

"You're still so young," she smarmed. "The whole world is your oyster, you know. Why settle for being an L.P.N. when you can earn an M.D. like John?"

John. Well aren't we chummy, she thought. And that last remark was precisely what she did not need to hear right now. Barbara's tone implied that nursing was on a par with flipping burgers for a living. But then, it was typical of the woman, whose tone and manner toward her, ever since Re-

ecca's mother had died, conveyed a sort of friendly, up-
beat pity that had always irked her.

Barbara was never so uncouth as to openly boast about
having snared a rich husband herself. But smug superiority
oozed from her tone: *Poor little orphan Becky, her mother
dead, her father might as well be for all the good he is.
Why, Hazel McCallum is practically the poor thing's only
parent.*

"As for me, I came to research the county archives,"
Barbara explained without being asked. "You may have
heard that the governor's wife has asked me to give the
annual address to the state historical society."

"How nice," Rebecca responded mechanically.

"Isn't it? But then again, I cannot really claim that I'm
all that surprised. The Wallants, you know, were among the
very first pioneers to settle the valley."

"Yes, I do know that," she replied, keeping the sarcasm
out of her tone only with an effort. She felt the real point
of the comment: the O'Reillys, in sharp contrast, didn't
arrive until the 1930s, penniless trash driven west by the
Great Depression.

"Hazel mentioned to me that your husband's family
worked for the McCallums way back when," Rebecca
added with secret pleasure at the momentary frown crum-
pling Barbara's brow. Edgar Wallant owned several thriving sawmills and like his wife hated the fact that even today
the McCallum name was worth more than theirs—and better respected. After all, Hazel hadn't denuded the area of
timber to make her fortune.

Now go ahead, Rebecca thought bitterly. Here's your
chance to really make my day. Bring up Louise and rub
my face in her success. It's what you're waiting to do. And
don't forget some catty little remark about John and Louise
while you're at it.

But Barbara didn't cut to the kill that quickly. She fell

in step beside Rebecca and entered the library foyer with her, a glassed-in expanse decorated with metal sculptures and trees in tub planters.

"Where did you study nursing, Becky?"

Barbara's smile showed too many teeth, and Rebecca realized Louise had inherited her horse grin from her mother. Also, however, good looks and a remarkable body.

"Colfax Community College," she replied, wishing this tiresome woman would just leave her alone.

"Well, it's quite affordable, I suppose," Barbara patronized her. "And conveniently located within driving distance. I've heard some people say that community colleges are nothing but high schools with ash trays. But that's unfair. You know, we sent Louise to Stanford. Personally, I think those big-name colleges are overrated. If you're smart, you'll do well anywhere, right?"

"Right," Rebecca repeated woodenly, wondering why she had to endure this insufferable humiliation on top of everything else she'd already experienced today.

"Well, anyway, I'd advise you to chat with Louise sometime," Barbara confided proudly. "Just last weekend she opened her newest bed and breakfast in Deer Lodge. Her fourth, you know. She has some impressive contacts in the medical community, by the way. Perhaps she could steer you in some more…lucrative direction."

Barbara knew good and well that her daughter and Rebecca would rather eat live worms than converse with each other. The suggestion was just another catty swipe at her, punishment for daring to reject membership in the Lady Wallant Admiration Society. However, she also felt a little nubbin of hope—despite that crack about "contacts in the medical community," at least Barbara wasn't mentioning John as specifically one of them.

"She hosted quite a celebration this weekend," Barbara added, and Rebecca felt a new pang of despair. That was precisely how John had looked on Monday morning—as if strung out from "celebrating."

Fortunately, by now they had pushed through the turnstile leading into the library proper. Since Barbara was still talking out loud, Rebecca pointed at the Quiet, Please sign.

"Well, I better get going," Rebecca whispered, heading quickly toward the return counter before Barbara could say anything else.

She knew she'd pay somehow for rudely brushing off a high-and-mighty Wallant like that, but right now Rebecca just didn't care. It was such a relief to be rid of her—an aching reminder of the "superior" people whose ranks were closed to her.

She dropped her overdue books in the return slot after paying a small fine on them. Then she crossed to the periodicals room and scanned the nation's major newspapers. Terrible drought in West Texas; crime down sharply in Los Angeles; alarming drop in the level of the Great Lakes...and terrible heartbreak in Mystery Valley, she thought in a welter of despair.

I just lost my virginity, she said to herself in a daze of confused wonder. And here I am, sitting in the library.

Is this it, then? For years you wonder what "it" will be like, and when it's over, it's *over?*

Abruptly the headlines in front of her began to shimmer, then melt, as tears of bitter disappointment filmed her eyes and splashed down her cold cheek.

Nine

Try as she might, Rebecca did not succeed at diverting her thoughts to the day's headlines. She gave up on the library and reluctantly headed back to her apartment.

Her cell phone had been turned off earlier. She'd had no heart for conversations with anyone. Now it burred almost immediately after she turned it back on. She picked it up off the seat as she drove out of the library parking lot.

"Hello?"

"Well cut off my legs and call me shorty," Hazel's deep, mellow voice greeted her. "I was beginning to think maybe our little hometown heroine had absconded with her employer. You all right, Becky?"

Oh, I'm just peachy, she thought in a moment of bitter self-pity. But she pushed that feeling aside and, with an effort to keep her tone normal, replied, "I'm fine. Just feeling those jet-lag blahs. We didn't finish up till daylight, and I'm not used to sleeping during the day. I'm driving back from the library now."

All more or less true, Rebecca thought, if she didn't count the lies by omission. However, Hazel must not have been entirely convinced.

"You sound a little...put-upon," the cattle queen suggested, fishing for the right word.

"Oh, it's nothing really, just lingering annoyance. I ran into Barbara Wallant at the library. You know how she can push my buttons."

"Shoo," Hazel scoffed. "Barbara Wallant is all hat and no cattle, you know that. Always flapping her gums about how she's a 'true native.' Native, my sweet aunt! Her husband's kin go way back to the homestead days, true. But *he* came out here from Fort Wayne, Indiana, when she was a kid. That surgically firmed butt of hers has never sat in a saddle."

"I know she's just a phony snob, but I just...well, I don't like to call her a witch, Hazel. But that's exactly what she is."

Rebecca's tone had grown sharper as she spoke, revealing her strong feelings. Hazel seemed to pause, evaluating the voice, before she replied.

"A witch with a snap-on halo," she agreed. "But I remember when she was younger. Edgar Wallant's hightoned wife has been kissed under the bleachers plenty of times. Tell me, though—is it really Barbara who gets your dander up? Or is it Louise?"

"They can *both* dry up and blow away for all I care. Thank God Louise is hardly ever around town anymore."

"What do you care about those two ditzes? You're a hometown hero."

"Oh, don't be silly. I just did my job."

"That right? Did nursing school require you to rappel down a cliff, or—"

"Hazel, I didn't 'rappel' down anything."

"The news broadcasters claim you did."

"Nobody even talked to us. I guess we left before the could swarm."

"We?"

"John and I."

"Mmm. So he's 'John' finally. Good, that's progress Somehow I suspect he's also stopped calling you Mis O'Reilly."

Some innuendo in Hazel's tone made Rebecca glad th older woman wasn't there to see her flush.

"Anyway," Hazel went on, "they're still showing a cli of you and him coming up over the berm with that poo lady. She's doing fine, by the way, in case you haven' heard."

"Good," Rebecca said, meaning it. But when she faile to add anything else, Hazel's voice became suspiciou again.

"How," she probed carefully, "are you and John gettin; along?"

"All right, I guess," Rebecca offered reluctantly. Sh had never been good at fibbing to Hazel, so she cast abou for something to say that was quite truthful. "Less frictio lately. In fact, last time I saw him, we were both very civi to each other."

"'Civil,' huh?" Hazel didn't sound too impressed "Honey, I'm 'civil' to IRS agents. Are you two at logger heads over something?"

Rebecca's best effort to keep her cool just wasn' enough. Bitter resentment, rising like flood water over dam, seeped into her tone. "Just how could we be at log gerheads, Hazel? I mean, if we were fighting with eac other, that would kind of imply that we were having som kind of relationship, wouldn't it? And we're not. I've give up on dating doctors after Brian. They're no good for m and that's that. Besides, don't you know that the code o noblesse oblige requires the royalty to refrain from bickering with their inferiors?''

Her sarcastic emphasis on *royalty* left no doubt as to just whom she meant.

''Royalty? Sweet love, John Saville hasn't got one elitist bone in that buff body of his.''

''Surely you jest? I'm just glad I don't believe in reincarnation, or I'd be convinced I was his scullery maid in an earlier life. This time around I'm up to nurse.''

''You headstrong young fool,'' Hazel told her, her tone kinder than the words. ''John no more considers himself royalty than I consider myself a belly dancer.''

''No offense, Hazel,'' she replied archly. ''But *I'm* the one who's around him all day. I think I can tell an elitist snob when I'm constantly snooted by one.''

''Oh, yeah, you're sharp as a bowling ball, all right,'' Hazel gibed. ''Must be all those men you've had.''

Anger gripped her, and Rebecca said nothing. She'd never hung up on Hazel in her life, but she was close to it now.

However, her friend added mercilessly, ''How long have you been in love with him?''

That tore it for Rebecca.

''Oh, sure, of course,'' she said into the phone. ''I mean, how could I *not* be in love with Mr. Perfection? After all, who am *I* to resist the young Adonis, God's gift to women? Why—I should be grateful for every crumb!''

''He *is* Adonis,'' Hazel retorted, ''and *you* are Aphrodite. The kids you two are going to have someday will be so good-looking they'll be traffic hazards. I hope you both work through this lovers' spat. Toodle-oo, hon, I've got yard work.''

Hazel's audacity, as usual, left Rebecca speechless.

But it didn't matter, because the rancher had already hung up.

''Lovers' spat,'' she repeated aloud, her tone dripping

irony. Hazel used to be so perceptive about people. Perhaps age was finally starting to muddle her thinking. *The kids you two are going to have someday...*

What a joke. So absurdly funny it was almost hysterical, Rebecca assured herself just before she burst into tears.

Rebecca found a new message waiting on her machine at home.

"Hi, Becky, this is Bonnie Lofton at the *Mystery Gazette*. Congratulations on your fine work at the accident scene. We think it's a great story, and we're just dying to get a front-page photo of you and Dr. Saville together at his clinic. We really need to get it today so it'll come out tomorrow while it's still timely news. Could you please call our office as soon as possible? The number is 555-8347."

Rebecca liked Bonnie, who was married to Roy Lofton, Mystery's only constable. With Bonnie as editor-in-chief, the *Gazette* had won several prestigious awards in journalism and was widely read throughout Mystery Valley and even much of the state.

But no way, she assured herself, was she posing with John Saville for a photo. At least for right now she'd rather have all her molars yanked out with a pair of pliers than have to face him.

However, even as she stewed, the phone rang.

She let the machine pick it up.

"Hi, again, it's Bonnie calling back to tell you I've reached Dr. Saville, and he's agreed to a photo shoot sometime early this evening at the medical office. I can't say he was eager, but I badgered until he caved in. I hate to ask you on such short notice, but we really need that photo soon in order to make tomorrow's paper. This is an important human interest story, and it would be a shame if the state TV networks cover it and we don't. So please give me a call back as soon as you get this. I appreciate it."

Oh, cripes, Rebecca thought as she rewound the message tape. Much as I hate to do this, I can't stiff Bonnie. So Dr. Saville wasn't too keen on the idea, either. Why should he be—he got what he wanted. Easy sex with no obligations…slam, bam, see ya, ma'am. He probably only agreed because he couldn't resist the publicity for himself.

Reluctantly she called Bonnie at the *Gazette* and agreed to show up at the medical office at 6:00 p.m. It still hadn't really sunk in yet how widely the Copper Mountain rescue mission was being reported. But she found out a bit later when she turned on the 5:00 p.m. Action Four news broadcast out of Helena.

By now the story no longer led the news, but it was still prominent. And sure enough, there was the footage of the tired young doctor coming over the berm with his patient—Rebecca and Dan Woodyard right behind him. So even though no reporter had caught them in time, obviously a cameraman did.

But the most riveting part of the broadcast was the brief footage from the intensive care recovery ward at Lutheran Hospital. The woman John had carried up, identified as Carol Brining, a retired schoolteacher from Michigan, was still weak and pale, but managed a plucky, grandmotherly smile from her hospital bed.

"There were heroes on that mountain," she assured the camera, "and that's why I'm alive today."

Rebecca turned the TV set off and started to get ready for the photo shoot. Though the story brought tears to her eyes, it also left her feeling even more insecure. After all, the Admirers of John Saville Society had enough members already. This would only ensure more.

"What Bonnie's hoping for," explained O'Neil Bettinger, the *Gazette* photographer, "is a good representative photo of you two doing something together, doctor and nurse stuff. You know, some task you normally collaborate on, whatever.''

The three of them stood in the empty waiting room, only O'Neil looking relaxed and comfortable. The awkward tension in the faces and manner of the other two, however, had nothing to do with the fact of being photographed.

O'Neil's innocent words nonetheless made Rebecca flush: *You two doing something together.*

''Well, we often confer over X-rays,'' John suggested after an awkward silence. ''Since Becky's basically supervising postop care after a patient's surgery, she needs to also understand the preoperative condition. So we get together and discuss it along with lab results and other tests.''

''Sure, sure, that sounds great,'' O'Neil approved, already planning out the photo aloud. ''We can hang an X-ray up on your light doohickey, then have you two on either side of it, both looking up at it in profile.''

John's gaze had avoided hers since she'd arrived—or so it seemed to Rebecca. Now, however, she caught him frankly checking her out. She'd dressed in a full skirt with a small waist and a crisp, white short-sleeved blouse. Her long hair was pinned flat on both sides of her head but cascaded down over her shoulder blades in back, unrestrained.

Their eyes met, held, but then he looked quickly away again, his face firming into a frown.

New doubts filled her.

By now they'd all moved back into examination room A, and John switched on the backlit X-ray reading screen.

''Perfect,'' enthused O'Neil, a short, balding, slightly hyper man in his middle forties, dressed in a garish plaid sport jacket. ''There's already an X-ray hanging there. That's a…jaw, isn't it?''

"Knee," John corrected him with a straight face.

"Knee. Sure, sure, I didn't look close," O'Neil muttered as he opened the top of his twin-lens reflex camera and took a quick light reading. "What's the deal on this one, Doc? Broken bone?"

"Well, this patient is a teenage athlete who severely extended the left knee and damaged some cartilage and ligaments. He'll be undergoing surgery with me and an orthopedic team to strengthen the knee without actually replacing the joint. It's called an interstitial buildup, done mostly in younger patients to restore full use of the joint. It was first developed in sports medicine."

"Huh, interesting. Okay, Doc, now act just like you would if you and Becky were conferring. By the way, shouldn't you be wearing a starched lab coat or something?"

"Not here at the office, no. But I wouldn't be wearing this, either," John admitted, unbuttoning his dark-blue suit jacket and laying it aside.

"Good, good," O'Neil encouraged as they pretended to confer. "Just keep that up while I move around the room and take a few different angles. Bonnie likes to have a choice."

By now Rebecca very much regretted agreeing to this. John was standing so close she could smell his aftershave lotion. Thank heaven she had the excuse of an X-ray to keep from looking at him.

O'Neil had moved farther back, out of hearing range, if they spoke in low tones.

"Guess you didn't plan on seeing me like this, huh?" John muttered in her ear.

"Nor you me," she replied with forced lightness. "If it's any consolation, I don't want to be here, either."

So I was dead right earlier today, John thought. She *did* hustle me out of her place. And now she's making sure I get the message that she's not interested in a repeat performance.

"Be brave," he muttered with sarcasm. "The ordeal will soon be over."

Her gaze cut momentarily to his face. She read contempt in his eyes. It stabbed her insides.

"Perfect," O'Neil pronounced again. "I shot half a roll of film. Bonnie should get a nice piece together with it."

Rebecca hardly even heard him, her pulse was so loud in her ears, surging like angry surf. After the shoot all she wanted to do was escape to her car before tears overwhelmed her again.

O'Neil made it to his vehicle first. She was about to open her door when John's voice arrested her.

"Becky!"

She looked back over her shoulder. He had to lock the front doors, so he'd been the last one out of the building. Now he stood in the gathering darkness, an indistinct form watching her.

Her heart cooled and froze into a ball of ice.

She didn't want another rejection like she'd had with Brian. She couldn't endure another set of hopes crushed and broken. She'd been foolish to have succumbed to John Saville simply for the fact that the rejection was sure to come. And she should have known it going in.

She was not his equal, not in social status, nor in education. He was a handsome doctor in the peak of his vigor. It was only natural that he would want to play the field for a few years more. He would need to take his time choosing the wife who would enhance his lifestyle and career. There was no reason to rush into a relationship and saddle himself with a nobody. He would never pick her. It was all so brutally obvious she couldn't believe how stupid she'd let herself be.

So fool me twice, shame on me, she thought bitterly to herself.

"Yes?" she asked him, her voice cool, pleasant and even.

"This morning—what happened between us, I—that is, we're only human, you know. These things can get out of hand, I suppose and—"

"Don't worry about it. I enjoyed it," she answered, her tone a model of detachment. "Sorry if you were disappointed. I don't have the experience of some women, you know."

"Are you kidding? In fact, I..."

But his words fell away. He stood there in silence. Just watching her.

"Good. I'm so happy that you were satisfied," she answered like a clerk at a counter. Then she got into her car and drove away.

She didn't once look back. Her heart hammered her ribs. Even now she meant what she'd just told him. It wasn't their lovemaking she regretted, only its horrid but oh-so-logical aftermath.

However, she suspected she knew what he had started to suggest in the parking lot: couldn't they perhaps continue a convenient little secret affair? A no-hassles sexual liaison. The good doctor could grab himself a "nooner" now and then, something to tide him over until he selected the proper rich debutante wife. Perhaps his weekend getaways with Louise, or whomever, weren't quite enough to contain his raging testosterone.

For a few awful moments she recalled the cold, impersonal note that Brian had sent her when he dumped her and left for his new practice outside New York City: "I'm not cut out for this provincial life. You like it here just fine among the cattle and rednecks you grew up with, but I want more out of life than this place can offer."

And even though John had chosen, for whatever secret reasons of his own, to settle here in Mystery Valley, he was probably the same arrogant, social-climbing creep Brian had proved to be.

"You can go straight to hell, John Saville," she announced out loud, a brittle smile on her face. But the defiance in her tone was a far cry from the aching despair in her heart.

Ten

"**G**irls, I just don't understand it for the life of me," Lucinda Shoemaker confided to Rebecca and Lois on Wednesday morning. "Several friends have told me, quite rudely, that my makeup is all wrong. And I could feel Dr. Saville staring at my face during our appointment. Should I perhaps try a different shade for the eyeliner?"

Lois had to struggle to keep a straight face, and normally Rebecca would have been cracking up, too. Lucy had a reputation as a harmless eccentric, and her downright ghoulish makeup jobs had been a standing joke around town for years now.

It was a shame, actually, because the fiftyish widow was quite attractive, with regal bone structure in her face. But her hideous war paint only scared away potential beaux.

This morning, however, Rebecca had no heart to join Lois in her mirth. Oddly, seeing the huge, full-color photo of John and her on the front page of this morning's *Mystery*

Gazette had only deepened her depression and made her regret posing for it. It seemed to mock her true plight by creating the impression they were a "good team." Which they were, medically speaking—but *only* medically speaking.

"Perhaps you need a better makeup light," Lois suggested, her tone tactful.

"Light?" Lucy blinked a few times while she tore a check from her leather wallet and handed it to Lois. "No lights on my vanity table, thank you. These days I apply my makeup by candlelight only, dear. After all, that's the light we gals need to look best in."

"By candlelight?" Lois repeated, astonished. Again her amused eyes met Rebecca's, and the latter had to force a grin.

Any other time, Rebecca would have found this admission absolutely hilarious. Today, however, nothing seemed funny.

"But if you apply it in candlelight," Lois explained, "it will clash horribly with other lighting. You can't truly tell how much you're putting on—especially rouge," she added in a not-so-subtle hint, for Lucy's cheeks were practically caked with it.

"Do you think so?" Lucy tried to sound politely interested, but a little sniff gave away her true skepticism. "If so, then it's up to the rest of the world to burn more candles. At my age others must compromise to keep the illusion of my beauty alive."

"It's not an illusion," Lois assured her. "You have beauty, all right. It's simply mismanaged."

After Lucy had left, still unconvinced her system was faulty, Lois turned her amazed face toward Rebecca.

"Do you believe that woman?" she demanded, convulsing in laughter.

"She's a space cadet, all right," Rebecca agreed, looking

up from a patient file on her computer screen and trying to muster a smile.

Her halfhearted acting, however, did not fool Lois. The latter had noticed all morning how worry molded Rebecca's face when she thought no one was looking.

"What's wrong?" Lois demanded with frank concern. "Usually Lucy makes you break up with laughter."

"I guess I'm still a little off-kilter from the accident Monday night," she fibbed. "You know, lost sleep and all that."

Lois was a good friend, not just a fellow employee, and Rebecca had often confided in her when troubles weighed on her mind. But right now she still felt overwhelmed with misery she couldn't even begin to discuss. She had returned to the office this morning to find the relaxed, affectionate John Saville of yesterday returned to his cold vinyl-boy self. It was weird, like being whisked back in time.

The complete reversion to his former personality made her feel even more uncomfortable with her memory of making love with him. Like a woman riding on a train who dreamed about a woman riding on a train, she felt confused about what was real and what was just imagination.

Only yesterday, yet it already seemed like a distant, blurry memory, not a recent event. At moments she could even believe it had never happened. As if she really had gone home alone and simply dreamed about making love with him.

Lois's voice jarred her back to the present. "Funny—the good doctor, too, is 'off-kilter' this morning."

"Oh? I hadn't noticed," Rebecca replied lamely.

Lois watched Rebecca from speculative eyes. "He hardly spoke when he came in, and he's been camped back in his office."

"Is that right?" Rebecca replied absently, feigning great interest in the patient history on her screen.

When sadness wasn't making her feel like weeping, anger made her want to march right back to his office and slap his face.

True, she had just recently been initiated into the ranks of those who'd had sex, but now she could see how the experience had temporarily washed away all her common sense. She now knew the most valuable lesson about men: they were wonderfully intense in the throes of lust, but then, their passion spent, they ran like a river when the snow melts.

The phone on Lois's half-moon desk burred.

"Dr. Saville's office," she answered. After listening a moment, she said, "No, this is the office number. Hang on and I'll transfer you to his private line."

Lois transferred the call. "'May I pleeeze speak with Jooohn?'" she repeated, exaggerating her enunciation. "This gal talks like a speech therapist to the nobility."

Rebecca paid little attention to her friend, busy finding the lab results John Saville had requested on one of his patients. She printed it out and headed back to his office. There was a file folder taped to his door; she was grateful she didn't have to face him.

She dropped the printout into the file and started to turn away.

Abruptly, however, John's voice rose a few decibels, as if in mild irritation.

"Look, sure I can make it this weekend. No problem. But *please* don't call me at the office. You've got my home number, haven't you?"

She felt a sharp pang behind her heart. It was the woman Lois had just transferred to his line. Louise Wallant had a precise, somewhat stilted enunciation, indicative of her snobbish, superior personality.

Misery crushed her all over again. The idea that John could make love to her yesterday, seeming to be so passionate, then set up another tryst for this weekend, was as devastating as she feared it would be. Nor could she fail to feel the irony of her present misery. In the beginning, his ''secret weekends'' had enhanced the mystique, the enigma this man seemed to be, as did his reluctance to talk about his past or what he was up to. In fact, it had been her curiosity about *who* the real Dr. John Saville was that first put her on the path to falling in love with him.

Now, however, she had the sinking conviction that the ''mystery man'' was simply slinking off to a clichéd sordid sexual liaison. Barbara Wallant's comment about the ''celebration'' for Louise's new bed and breakfast opening up only strengthened Rebecca's conviction.

Even in the depths of her despair, however, she cautioned herself against putting the noose before the gavel, as Hazel called it. She already knew John was spending weekends with Louise, for example. How could she blame him now for something that was going on before she had even met him?

She returned to the front office, still lost in the moil of troubled, conflicting thoughts.

''I wonder,'' Lois speculated, ''who that is on the phone? She wasn't trying to make an appointment.''

''Who cares who she is?'' Rebecca snapped, clearing her computer screen.

Astonished, Lois stared at her for a long moment, her eyes narrowing at her friend's tight-lipped frown.

''Evidently,'' she replied in a mild tone, ''one of us cares very much.''

Toward the end of Wednesday afternoon, Hazel went out back to the main barn to check on Pavlov's cows as she called the Lazy M's experimental breeds.

She flicked a toggle switch mounted on a panel, and the big front doors slid open on their greased tracks. The smell of cows and sweet new hay wafted to her nostrils. Mellow sunlight flooded inside, making tiny dust motes glitter like galaxies and revealing a long, twin row of stalls.

"Hello, Marie," she called out, stopping beside one of the stalls.

The cow watching her from placid, pretty brown eyes had been given a French name in honor of her breed, the cream-colored French Charolais, popular for crossbreeding since the 1930s. Hazel's first ancestors had bred only the tough and self-sufficient longhorn cattle, driven north from deep in Texas and first brought to America by Spanish explorers. Later had come the shorthorn, the white-faced Hereford, the black Aberdeen Angus and several others. Hazel was trying every possible crossbreeding combination to produce heartier animals and better-quality meat.

"Well, the bull has done his job, Mama," she said, patting the animal's broad brow. "Now you're preggers, and Hazel's gonna be with you all the way. We're going to deliver a healthy calf, and I'll be there at your side when you lick its eyes open."

Most people assumed cows were stupid, but Hazel had seen how they learned to bond with humans. When her line riders came down from summer pasture and separated from the herd after four months with them, the critters just stood there and bawled for hours, they missed the cowboys so. And a few honest cowboys even admitted they missed the cows, too.

"I can make a cow love a cowboy," she thought aloud, "but I'm having six sorts of trouble pairing Becky with John. Maybe I've lost my touch as a master matchmaker, Marie."

As she turned to go back outside, however, Hazel's glance fell on the tack-room door at the far end of the barn. And suddenly, just like that, the rough outline of a plan sprang into her mind—followed by a wide, mischievous grin on her weather-seamed face and a canny twinkling in her Prussian-blue eyes.

"It'll have to be my last-ditch effort," she told herself. "But if all else fails, I'll give it a shot."

Those two stubborn, hard-headed youngsters belonged together, she was still sure of it. They just didn't know it yet, was all. And after all, hadn't she succeeded in the difficult case of rodeo champ A. J. Clayburn and Southern socialite Jacquelyn Rousseaux? Those two got along like cats fighting, at first. Now they were expecting their second child and still acted like newlyweds on their honeymoon.

And she'd played Cupid to her dear friend Connie Adams. She sure hadn't expected to snare her a renegade lawman, but all in all Quinn Loudon made Connie a mighty fine match, and Hazel liked to think she had a reining hand in that happiness, too.

These thoughts reminded her the workday was over and that John Saville might be at home by now.

Think I'll give him a call, she decided, and see if he'll give me a ride in that fancy race car of his. That handsome young fool needed another lesson in how to spark a woman, and she meant to tutor him until he got it right.

Besides that, she had a question to ask him about something very curious she had just learned today.

"So how are you feeling, Hazel?" John asked, holding the Alfa Romeo's passenger door open for her.

"I'm right as the mail," she assured him, spryly lowering herself into the brown leather seat. "It's mighty nice of you to agree to give me a ride in this beauty. I've been wanting to ever since I first laid eyes on her."

"Heck, you can drive if you want."

"Thanks, but this way I can look around more. It's a beautiful day."

"Well, you don't need to thank me. I was glad you called—I can use a relaxing drive myself."

He closed her door, crossed to his side and got in, then fired the old race car's engine to rumbling life.

"Got a lot on your mind?" she inquired with seemingly casual interest as they followed the Lazy M's long, meandering driveway. Hazel, her hair restrained by a scarf of poppy-colored silk sewn with sequins, waved at a few hands who had stepped out of the bunkhouse to admire the gleaming red classic auto.

John's cobalt eyes glanced at her for a moment before he answered.

"Professionally speaking, not really. But personally speaking," he admitted, "I sure have plenty on my mind."

"Now, now, Doctor, I don't like that tone. Might get you sick."

"Get a horse, Doc!" one of the cowboys shouted as they drove past, and John tooted the horn at him.

They were out on the main road now, and he raised his voice above the throbbing roar of the exhausts. "Hey who's the doctor here?" he objected playfully.

"You're the medical doctor. But you're only thirty and I'm...well, a woman of a certain age. That makes me the doctor of philosophy."

His strong white teeth flashed in a grin. "I guess it does at that. And don't play coy with me, I know your age exactly. You told me yourself you were born the same year this car rolled off the assembly line. And you're running just as strong."

"If you take Canyon Drive," she suggested, "we'll be able to see the entire valley at sunset. The view takes your breath away. I haven't seen it for years from up in the mountains."

"Then Canyon Drive it is." John downshifted and turned

left onto a smaller asphalt road that ascended into the nearby granite peaks in a series of looping switchbacks.

Hazel knew, of course, that it was Rebecca who weighed on the young man's mind. But she also knew that men, unlike women, were not as comfortable discussing those feelings closest to their hearts. So she decided to come at her real topic indirectly.

"I found out something very interesting today," she remarked casually. "You see, one of my favorite charities is the Montana State Native American Scholarship Fund. They just sent me a wonderful letter thanking me for my annual contribution. And lo and behold, among the names on the letterhead, the honorary board members, I see a Dr. John Saville."

He nodded. "Yep. I've been on the board for five years now."

"Well, good for you. It's a wonderful organization. Native Americans in Montana haven't prospered as well as some tribes elsewhere. The McCallums, you know, intermarried with the Northern Cheyenne, and I'm one-eighth Indian myself. In fact, that's where I get my stunning good looks. Do you have Indian blood, too?"

He shook his head. "No, but I might as well have. I have strong childhood ties to the Blackfoot Tribe in the Bitterroot Valley. My dad spent the last years of his Army career at the fort near the reservation, then he retired in the area. I lived there from the time I turned ten years old until I went off to college. Most of my friends in school were from the reservation."

Hazel watched a cloud seem to cross his face as he alluded to those days. It's not his friends he doesn't like to talk about, she realized. He had mentioned his connection to the tribe with real pride in his voice. But he sure never volunteers any information about that father of his, she thought sympathetically. Children from happy families were usually eager to talk about their parents.

By now Canyon Road had leveled out high above the verdant valley. Near at hand they could see canyon walls marked with striation; farther below, the valley meadows were brilliant with blue columbine and white Queen Anne's lace.

"Does Becky," Hazel inquired with an exaggerated lack of guile, "know anything about your background?"

"She knows my dad was career military."

"Is that all you've told her?"

The peaceful look instantly deserted John's handsome face, replaced by a resentful frown. "You kidding? If I told her much more, she'd run. She has a pretty high opinion of herself, and she isn't shy about keeping me at a distance."

Hazel shook her head in amazement at this younger generation. "Oh, land love us. You two take the cake."

"Hell, she doesn't have to worry about me. I'll be happy to go out of my way to leave her precious freedom alone," he insisted, angry hurt working into his tone.

"Maybe that's your mistake," Hazel put in mildly.

But by now he was getting too worked up to notice.

"Pretty girls are a dime a dozen," he stormed on. "She doesn't have to act like she's the Hope Diamond or something. Serious, down-to-earth men like me are probably just too boring for—"

"John," Hazel cut in sharply.

"Huh?"

"Quit flapping your gums, would you, and listen for a minute?"

A sheepish color touched his cheeks. "Yeah. I guess I'm getting a little carried away, aren't I?"

They've made love, Hazel gloated, knowing without having to ask. There's a good chance here, after all, if I can just get these two young fools to shake off their blinders.

"First of all," she told him firmly, "all you're doing right now is blowing off a lot of hot air. You don't understand Becky any more than you understand a high-strung horse. And *she* doesn't understand you. Second of all, *you're* the man and you need to start acting like it. This is no time to go puny and be on the defensive. When it comes to love, rearguard actions won't get it done. Not with a lass like Becky. You know the old saying—faint heart never won fair lady. And Becky is definitely a fair lady, wouldn't you agree?"

John mustered a woebegone smile. "'The fairest flower in all the fields,'" he conceded.

"Well, instead of quoting Shakespeare to *me,* lay the sweet nothings on her."

One of his hands balled into a fist on the steering wheel. "It's more complicated than that, Hazel, she—"

"Oh, complicate a cat's tail, you gorgeous idiot. When you're neither up the well nor down, you *must* make a move. Fight or show yellow, young man."

"Maybe I'm just yellow, then," he confessed coldly.

"Uh-huh, sure you are. I s'pose the man who carried that injured schoolteacher up the side of Copper Mountain was a coward?"

"That was different."

"How? It showed what kind of mettle you have in you when push comes to shove. As my great-granddad Jake McCallum would've put it, you'll do to take along."

By now the day was waning, and a copper sunset flared in the west. They were headed back down into the valley.

"Hazel," John said after a few minutes of reflective silence, "you *are* a doctor of philosophy. I'll be thinking about what you've said. I don't disagree with you. It's just…things are always simpler in theory than they are in fact.''

Hazel nodded. ''I know that,'' she conceded. ''A cattle drive is easy to plot on the map but a hell-buster on the trail. But you have to ask yourself one question and only one—Is she worth the effort? When you have the answer to that one, you can go forward.''

He was silent. His jaw tightened as they turned into the driveway of the Lazy M in the gathering twilight.

''Thank you for the ride,'' she said as John hopped out and went around to open her door.

''Be patient with Becky,'' she counseled him by way of a parting injunction. ''She has a streak of Irish temper, so take her unpleasant comments with a grain of salt.''

''Tell me, Dr. McCallum,'' John quipped, ''do I take that grain of salt on an empty or full stomach?''

They both shared a smile as Hazel opened the side door of her sprawling ranch house. She planted a quick kiss on his cheek.

''Just try to relax and be as warmly humorous around her as you are with me,'' she assured him. ''Open up a little and let her know you aren't who and what she *thinks* you are.''

''I will try,'' he promised. ''But I'm not optimistic.''

''There are always other fillies in the field, Doc. It's you who has to decide. Is she worth it? Answer that, and the rest is easy.''

He nodded. The look in his eyes grew pensive, then hardened into an emotion that looked to Hazel very much like resolve.

Eleven

Rebecca had spent much of Wednesday evening fretting about the brief fragment of phone conversation she'd heard outside John's office door: *Look, sure I can make it this weekend. No problem. But please don't call me at the office. You've got my home number, haven't you?*

Barbara Wallant's talk about a celebration in Deer Lodge last weekend; John's worn-out appearance on Monday morning; his secret weekends; and now the overheard phone call twisted her heart dry. That he'd made love to her after a hedonistic weekend with Louise—or anyone else—left her torn between sheer outrage and emotional devastation.

Plagued by visions of withered spinsterhood, she had finally drifted off to sleep long after midnight. But her sleep was troubled by unpleasant dreams. The one that disturbed her most took place in the office.

In her dream, O'Neil was once again taking their photo

for the *Gazette*. Only this time when Rebecca glanced up at the X-ray on the screen, it turned into a torrid photo of John and Louise, naked, wrapped in each other's arms.

With the dream still plaguing her thoughts, she drove to work on Thursday morning in a foul mood, ready for a clash with her employer. Instead, to her surprise and relief, John's manner and behavior toward her—even in front of Lois—was affectionate, respectful, even deferential.

"Good morning, ladies," he greeted both of them cheerfully the very moment he showed up at 8:30 a.m.

Instead of going right back into his private office, as he usually did, to read medical journals and await the day's first patient, he remained up front to chat with them.

"Which one of you picked these?" he inquired, nodding toward the wicker baskets brimming with fresh pink-and-white azaleas.

"Becky," Lois answered promptly. "Hazel calls her the flower girl because she's always got to have them close by. She always leaves a little early to pick the flowers for the office."

"They come from Hazel's meadows," Rebecca put in. "I asked her if it's okay."

His smile and sexy, intensely blue eyes, seemed to drink her in. She had worn a rose silk blouse with a deep slit skirt that revealed a shapely calf—shapely in her employer's opinion, judging from his prolonged glance.

"Thank you, Becky, they're beautiful," he assured her, still holding that charming, warm smile. "Not that this office is lacking for beauty."

She flushed at the unexpected compliment. It was probably just banal lip service from the mouth of a gigolo, but still, her thirsty soul cried out for his flirtations.

"Well, now," commented an equally surprised Lois after

their boss went back to his office. "What was *that* all about?"

"Better ask him," Rebecca said, deflecting the question. She was busy at her computer station, calling up medical histories on all of the day's appointments. It gave her an excuse to avoid Lois's scrutiny. But in fact she still felt so rattled by John's charm just now that she could hardly focus on the screen.

"I don't need to ask him," Lois declared with assurance. "I know all about boys, remember? I'm surrounded by them. You ask me, our brilliant young surgeon has either won the lottery or he's in love."

"You can conclude that from one kind remark?" Rebecca challenged, her skepticism genuine.

"No, it was more in the look he gave you, Becky. You know, the famous look that speaks volumes."

"You're just an incurable romantic," Rebecca scoffed. "And considering the kind of guy you're married to, I can see why. You two just celebrated your twentieth anniversary, and Merrill still treats you as if you guys just started dating. Candy, flowers, holds the door for you."

"I'll keep him around," Lois agreed. But Rebecca's obvious diversion had not fooled her. "Tuesday," she added, "when you two took the day off—did you perhaps spend it together?"

"Ask me no questions," Rebecca demurred, "and I'll tell you no lies."

A wide smile divided the older woman's pleasant face. "Oh, I think my question's been adequately answered, thank you."

A few minutes later, however, Rebecca felt her new, improved mood back-pedaling a bit. She had just noticed who today's 2:00 p.m. appointment was—Janet Longchamps, a familiar and unwelcome name from her high school days. Janet and Louise Wallant were both seniors when Rebecca was a junior, the two of them tight as ticks. Like Louise, Janet came from a wealthy family, her father being one of the state's real estate mandarins. Janet had gone off to an exclusive college back East, earning her MRS. degree when she married a wealthy product-liability lawyer. Divorced after only one year of marriage, childless, she had returned to Mystery Valley to lead whatever social scene there was in cattle country.

There was no file under her name on the computer menu, Rebecca quickly verified. Meaning that this was her first appointment with John.

"Did Janet Longchamps say what her problem was when she made an appointment?" she asked Lois. "Her curable problem, I mean?"

"Nary a peep. Just requested a consultation. Maybe she wants her nose lifted higher into the air," Lois joked. "Or her nose cones."

They both laughed, for Janet's trademark combination of low-cut bodice and push-up bra left little to the imagination.

But Janet's crassness aside, the appointment niggled at Rebecca. John was neither a G.P. nor a gynecologist, but an expensive surgeon. Yet, it sure seemed as if plenty of young, healthy, rich women suddenly wanted to "consult" with him.

That's not his fault, she reminded herself. He's rich and good-looking, so naturally some of the available women are drawn to him like flies to syrup. The woman who marries him will have to have the patience of a martyr.

The woman who marries him. Those words now troubled her more than she wanted to admit. She had assumed, upon first meeting him, that he would make some woman a fine husband when he finally met the woman he wanted.

Unfortunately for her, it wouldn't be her. She still had to remain cool and unentangled. His charm today flared her secret hopes. Nonetheless, she lectured herself sternly, you can't start expecting miracles every time he smiles sweetly at you. And you definitely can't freak out every time some willowy socialite like Janet requests a "consultation." He's single, she told herself again and again. You have no hold on him whatsoever.

She glanced up from her computer and saw Lois watching her with a knowing grin.

"What?" she demanded defensively, feeling heat come into her face.

Lois laughed. "Would you look at Nurse Becky blush. Things are starting to get mighty interesting around here."

At 1:30 p.m. Lois left for a dental appointment, Rebecca having agreed to cover the phone and reception duties for her. With no patient scheduled until Janet arrived at two, Rebecca decided to ready the next pickup for the lab courier who stopped by each afternoon.

She was seated at the front desk, recording sample ID numbers into a ledger, when John came up front from his office.

"Mail come yet?" he asked, flashing a smile at her.

"It usually doesn't get here until two or two-thirty," she replied, returning the smile.

"Oh. Okay."

She was pretty sure he already knew that. And he made no movement to leave, just standing there in the doorway watching her. It occurred to her that the mail was a pretext to get a conversation started.

Instead of resuming her task, she pushed the sample tray aside and widened her smile, encouraging him.

"We're hardly ever alone like this," he said awkwardly. "I mean, now that we've..."

"Become friends?" she asked with forced lightness and charm.

He looked at her. Whatever he wanted to say, it wa
evidently costing him an effort. He shrugged. She watche
his shirt tighten around his biceps and shoulders when h
did.

"You sure are in good shape," she said, resorting t
compliments in order to avoid the pain. "No wonder yo
were able to carry that teacher up the mountain."

His eyes took in all of her in one lingering, smolderin
look.

A mutual, awkward silence deepened.

He opted for a burst of candor. "Look, can I ask you
very personal question?"

"Seeing as how we've both already been 'very personal'
with each other," she replied, "I don't think it's a prob
lem."

"How in the world could a woman like you still be
virgin?"

She gave him a brittle laugh. "You forgot to add 'unti
recently.'"

"You know where I'm going here. I mean, there mus
have been plenty of guys who were more than eager t
change that fact."

"Maybe I was just too picky," she said, her eyes turning
away. "But maybe it never felt quite like the right time.'

His intense eyes held her gaze. "Tuesday? Did that fee
like the right time?"

She grew silent, wrestling with her out-of-control emo
tions. Taking a deep breath, she said, "Look, I can't say i
was the right time. It just felt right, so I did it. Hey, it wa
long overdue. It's really not a big deal. Happens every day
to some woman, I assure you."

He hesitated, then spoke what was on his mind. "I guess
I wasn't really sure if...well, you know. I wasn't sure i
you just had a moment of weakness, and maybe I sort o
unfairly exploited it."

"If so," she assured him coolly, logically, completely avoiding her true feelings, "then we both did. You were the innocent one, after all. If I was so worried about being a 'good girl,' I could've made up a bed on the floor."

"I'm glad you didn't."

"Sure. Same here." She tried to shrug off his conversation and go back to her work, but her mistake was to look at him.

His stare held her spellbound.

"I'll tell you what," he said, "if I'd woken up first, I'd've joined you on the floor."

Like a magnet pulling on steel, he drew steadily closer. He placed his hands on the desk, and drew down, until his lips barely brushed hers.

The kiss was testing, inquisitive, hungry, even while his posture was dominant and pressing. His mouth invited, his body language possessed. The contact was electric.

She stared up at him, her insides melting as desire sent her pulse thrumming through her veins.

He leaned down again and answered her wordless invitation. His strong surgeon's hand cupped her chin and his lips covered hers in a soul-probing kiss.

Time stood still. For sweet precious seconds, Rebecca surrendered to him; to the enticing taste of his insistent mouth, to the dark pheromonal scent of his maleness that clung to his skin like a drug that had been concocted for her pleasure alone. He deepened the kiss with his tongue, probing, licking, consuming. She tugged on his bottom lip with her teeth, affirming his sexual onslaught with her answer.

Gone was all her cool logic and prudence. She wanted more of him, hell, she wanted all of him. And she wanted him now. Her feelings for him went core deep. She couldn't ever see it going away, not when she was fifty, or eighty, or when she married another man and had his children.

Some needs lasted a lifetime, and she was beginning to see that what he had sparked in her was destined only to be quenched by him.

She released a small moan when he broke away. Loneliness and greed for him rushed back like an ill wind she wanted gone.

"Does this mean," he whispered against her hair, his voice husky with desire, "I wouldn't be out of line if I asked you out?"

Before she could reply, however, the door in the foyer sprang open. He straightened and just barely managed to put a respectable distance between them before Janet Longchamps' statuesque form appeared in the waiting room—fifteen minutes early, Rebecca noted with a stirring of resentment and irritation.

"I'm a weensie bit early, Dr. Saville," she called out with that magisterial nuance of tone Rebecca remembered from high school. "Don't worry about me, I'll just flip through a magazine until you're ready to see me."

So far she hadn't seemed to recognize—or even notice—Rebecca. That treatment had begun even before Rebecca's mother died and she became "poor little Becky O'Reilly, Hazel McCallum's favorite charity." Janet and Louise were horrified that she actually had to baby-sit and do other jobs to pay for simple little things like her school photos and senior class ring.

Janet radiated that limitless confidence Rebecca had noticed among some who came from wealthy backgrounds. Tall, designer clad, perfectly poised, she moved across the empty waiting room with the hypnotic grace of a model on a fashion runway.

Rebecca could not blame John for staring at her, for she herself was also getting an eyeful of Janet. She wore a sexy black knit dress that clung to her svelte, aerobically fine-tuned figure like plastic wrap. Platinum-blond bangs were feathered over her forehead. When she demurely settled into a leather-and-chrome chair, she crossed long legs, setting them off to perfection.

"I'll be ready in a couple minutes," John called out to Janet, giving Rebecca a long deep stare. "I just need to download something on my computer. Becky will have a few routine background questions for you first." He left reluctantly for his office.

Only now, when they were alone, did Janet deign to finally notice Rebecca. She studied her for a few moments as if she were a zoo animal Janet couldn't quite remember.

"I recognize you," she abruptly announced as if she deserved jewels in heaven. Her tone was off-putting if not quite rude. "Becky O'Reilly."

A mechanical smile was the best Rebecca could muster. "Hi, Janet. I haven't seen you in, what, almost six years, I guess."

She wasn't sure if that odd contortion of Janet's mouth was a smile or a smirk. "Yes, since high school. I was away at Holyoke for several years, then I got married and lived in Boston briefly. Now I'm divorced," she added as if that were the natural course of things among Those Who Are. "And I'm back in the valley. My father is teaching me the real estate business. So...you've become a receptionist?"

"Actually I'm a nurse. Just filling in up front."

"I see," Janet replied as if it hardly mattered to her what the hoi polloi chose to do. She had been just as indifferent toward Rebecca when they were in school together. Janet's time was spent on social activities like cheerleading and governing her exclusive clique, which had included Louise Wallant. Rebecca had excelled, on the other hand, at academics and spent her free time helping Hazel and riding horses at the Lazy M.

Rebecca took out the standard medical history form required of all first-visit patients.

"I just need to ask you a few—"

"Oh, save yourself the trouble, Becky," Janet cut her off rudely. "I'm not here for any medical problem."

Rebecca's strained smile wilted at the rude, dismissive tone. "But this is a *medical* office. Why have you requested an appointment?"

"Don't worry, I'm paying for it. I had to come into town, anyway, to show a property, so I figured I'd chat up Dr. Saville while I'm here. I know he's busy, so I figured an appointment was the best bet."

Chat up, Rebecca thought with disdain. Just as pretentious as she'd always been. Hazel's words about Barbara Wallant now occurred to her: *She's all hat and no cattle.*

"I saw his photograph in yesterday's newspaper. He's quite a handsome and distinguished-looking man for one so young."

"Yes," Rebecca replied, keeping her tone carefully level. "I was in that photo, too."

Janet's eyes widened in surprise. "Oh, was that other person you? I must have read the caption too quickly. Besides, you look much different today without your uniform."

I wasn't *wearing* a uniform, Rebecca almost pointed out, then thought better of it. Why bother? Egocentric Janet couldn't care less.

Behind her, she heard John open his office door, signifying that he was ready to see his patient.

"You can go on back now," Rebecca told her, restraining herself from adding, *But why don't you go to hell instead?*

She half expected the visit to end quickly, for John was pretty much all business when it came to medicine. He surely wouldn't appreciate this frivolous use of office time for obvious socializing.

But she was wrong. Before very long, peals of laughter—masculine and feminine—reached her in the front office. And a lively conversation was ensuing, although she couldn't hear their actual words.

Well, let's just close down the office and have a party, she fumed, anger replacing the warmth and closeness she had just begun to feel with John. All it took was the arrival of a "pert skirt" with a bankroll to turn the guy into a medical playboy.

But even as her fury mounted with each new peal of mirth, she cautioned herself against giving in to jealousy. It was her own fault she was miserable. She had no business having a fling with her employer. Cool and detached were the only ways to go and she had almost slipped up again with his unexpected kiss.

While she was ruminating, the postman dropped the day's mail through the slot.

She crossed the waiting room and knelt to pick it up, rolling the rubber band off and starting to sort through it as she returned to the reception desk. A few medical-supply catalogs, a bill for the new air conditioner, a couple of payment envelopes...

She stopped a few steps from the desk, staring at a vellum-finish envelope with fancy, gold-embossed letters in the upper lefthand corner:

Louise Wallant
17 Congress Street
Deer Lodge, Montana

In one keenly disappointing moment, Rebecca felt her newfound hope eroding. She had just finished lecturing herself about being unfair regarding Janet; now this new blow caught her with no defenses left.

What I told Hazel about reincarnation was wrong, she thought. I wasn't John's maid in an earlier life; I was the maid to his rich girlfriends.

For a moment she actually envisioned herself drudge-capped and aproned, dropping a servile curtsy as John disappeared behind bedroom doors, Janet on one arm, Louise on the other. She was still holding that unwelcome image when the doctor and his visitor appeared in the front office again, still engrossed in their chat.

Again Janet didn't even deign to notice her, as if she were merely a piece of furniture. And John's behavior toward his wealthy visitor— Anger knotted Rebecca's insides as she noticed how easy, confident and relaxed he'd become, Lothario with a stethoscope, natural-born seducer of socialites.

That glib mouth of his, she realized with a sinking feeling, had just kissed her own lips.

However, Rebecca kept her anger out of her face and manner as Janet left, not even bothering to say goodbye to her.

John, still smiling from the visit, turned to his nurse again.

"As I recall—" he picked up their curtailed conversation "—you and I were arranging a date."

She had resumed her task of recording lab samples in the ledger. Before he could say anything else, she spoke up. "All right. How about this coming weekend? Saturday night's good for me."

Just as she had feared, a frown settled onto his handsome features. "I'm tied up this weekend."

Tied up, she thought sarcastically. Gets kinky at Louise's, does it?

"Oh?" she replied demurely. Her eyes cut to the stack

of mail she'd put on Lois's desk. Louise's letter sat atop the stack and seemed to stare back at her—mockingly so.

She waited to see if he would offer any further explanation as to how he might be "tied up."

The lull became painful, then excruciating, as he simply stood there and said nothing.

"What about weekend after next?" he suggested. "Or during the week, would that be okay?"

She suddenly felt both crushed and infuriated that he would actually schedule her in as one of his concubines like a raja managing his harem. And *this* was the callous creep she'd surrendered her virginity to?

"I'll tell you what," she offered in icy tones, "how 'bout when I'm in the mood, I'll call you."

His mouth fell open in astonishment.

Before he could respond, the front door swung open and Lois appeared. She took one look at Rebecca's angry features, then at John's dumbfounded face.

"Ooops," Lois said, realizing she'd arrived at an awkward moment. "Should I go run an errand or two?"

"No," Rebecca answered firmly for both of them. "Our conversation is terminated."

I took Hazel's advice, John stewed later that evening while his frozen lasagna dinner thawed in the microwave. I wasn't defensive, I showed warmth and all that good stuff. And where did it get me? Becky turned on me like a rabid animal.

A late-spring cold front had moved in from Canada after sunset, and he had built up a small fire in the living room's big fieldstone fireplace. The house had been partially furnished when he'd purchased it, but he had gotten rid of the ugly embossed-plush sofa and the rest of the mass-produced furnishings that had rendered the room functional and tasteless.

He hadn't yet found time, however, to replace the stuff he'd tossed out, and the big house had an empty, cavernous feel. But he had kept the quaint lamps with parchment shades, and he had kept the sheer curtains and buffalo-check overdrapes.

Right now, however, he couldn't care less about decor. Not when the memory of his clash with Becky still smarted like an open wound.

Out in the kitchen the timer on the microwave dinged, letting him know supper was ready. But he simply sat motionless in the room's only armchair, trying to figure out what he had done wrong.

Shallow socialites like Janet Longchamps were predictable to him—they had been throwing themselves at him since his medical school days. But unique women like Becky stymied and intimidated him, for she was far more complex, far less manipulable.

He stared at the telephone on the mantel, trying to work up the courage to call her.

But anger, and a newly constructed wall of defensiveness, killed his impulse. By following Hazel's advice, he had taken a considerable emotional risk. And when she just turned on him like she did, Becky only confirmed his instinct to stay on the defensive with her.

Failure is not an option, his father's voice still echoed in memory.

His gaze lifted above the crackling, sawing flames to the decorative centerpiece of the room, mounted in a glass-fronted case: a beautifully carved, painted and decorated Blackfoot warrior coup stick.

It had been presented to him in a special council meeting of the tribe elders at their reservation located in the Bitterroot Valley, between Montana and Idaho. It was not a replica, but the genuine article from the glory days of the early nineteenth century, one of the most highly prized possessions of the tribe.

Fifteen brightly dyed feathers were tied to it, one for each time the warrior had ''counted coup'' on an enemy—touched the enemy or his horse with the stick. Anyone could kill from a distance, Indian warriors had reasoned, including a coward. But it took even more courage and risks to come close enough to actually touch a foe. In fact, a coup was far more honored than taking a life.

Risks...

Again John stared at the telephone. He took great pride in that coup stick, for it meant he was one of the few outsiders to be taken into the heart of the tribe. Yet, could he find the courage now to count coup on Becky, to move in close and touch her again despite the emotional risks?

He almost stood up and crossed to the telephone.

But then he reminded himself that it wasn't just a matter of courage. He had done nothing to merit her coldness today. If she wasn't interested in him, then that was her choice. He couldn't force her to want him.

Anger and resentment stirred within him, steeling his resolve to just forget about her.

Hazel, he decided, was a good and fascinating woman with her heart in the right place. Unfortunately, she just didn't understand Becky's personality.

''*You* can go to hell, too, Rebecca O'Reilly,'' he declared out loud in the big, nearly empty room.

And that, he assured himself, is my final word on it.

Twelve

Friday at the medical office was an excruciating ordeal for Lois, who was forced to witness two stubborn, prideful fools obviously trying to deny their love and attraction for each other.

The stiff, uncomfortable formality between John and Rebecca was back with a vengeance. It was ''Dr. Saville'' and ''Miss O'Reilly'' again, and while both of them still had plenty of smiles and kind words for the patients or Lois, with each other they could barely manage to be civil.

Twice Lois had to diplomatically intercede to prevent them from going at each other hammer and tongs over completely trivial matters.

Because she had been at the dentist's yesterday when the latest trouble storm brewed, Lois wasn't sure exactly what the problem was. By now, however, she and Hazel had become allies of a sort for this latest matchmaking campaign. So on Friday afternoon, when John stepped out of the office to grab a sandwich, and Rebecca was busy putting supplies away in the storeroom, Lois made a quick phone call to Hazel.

"Code Red," she informed the rancher, keeping her voice down so Rebecca wouldn't overhear her. "It's getting ugly, Hazel. Our two lovebirds are now involved in a full-fledged cockfight."

"What happened?" Hazel demanded.

"I wish I knew. Things were humming along just fine yesterday before I left for my dental appointment. By the time I got back, full-scale war had erupted."

Hazel expelled a long sigh at her end. "Has Becky said anything to you?"

"Zip. And when I asked her what was wrong, she just gave me the ugliest frown and said, 'Nothing a good hit man couldn't fix.'"

"Hmm…can't call that very promising—or can we? Obviously, some deep feelings are involved here, just not the right ones. Well, I'll run my traps. You got any hunches?"

"Well, there *was* a letter from Louise Wallant on top of the mail stack when I came back. And John's taking off again this weekend."

"That's better than a hunch," Hazel assured her. "I'll bet you just put your finger right on the problem."

"*Is* he driving to Deer Lodge weekends to see Louise?"

"Maybe. I understand they did have an affair at one time. But unless I read him all wrong, I just can't see him and Louise making beautiful music together."

"Same here," Lois agreed. "Uh-oh, I hear her coming, gotta go."

"Thanks for the report," Hazel told her just before they both hung up. "I'll work on her this weekend, though I confess I'm beginning to have my doubts about these two."

* * *

Saturday turned out to be a gloomy, cheerless day that perfectly matched Rebecca's mood. While the rain seemed to be holding off, not even a narrow seam of sunshine appeared in a cloudy sky the color of dirty bathwater.

She was up and dressed by 8:00 a.m. Although she had no appetite, she forced herself to eat a croissant with her morning coffee. But it was impossible to hang around her place—not with the sense of John's presence still so strong there.

She needed some busywork, so she decided to wash clothes. Since her apartment was too small for a washer and dryer, she had to drive to the laundromat in Mystery.

After I finish that, she resolved, *I think I'll go apartment hunting.*

She had purposely kept her small efficiency apartment, even though she could afford a roomier place, mainly because she knew Brian had been embarrassed by it. She'd refused to let a self-centered creep like him determine her lifestyle. But now it contained echoes she didn't want to hear anymore, and she no longer cared about her pride. She just wanted out.

Out. As she watched the hypnotic tumbling of her clothes in the dryers, that word kept gnawing at her. Out of her old apartment—and why not out of her job, too? After all, as bitterly unhappy as she felt, there was really no other solution.

For one thing, those weekend disappearances of John's, which once intrigued her, now made her feel very differently since they'd made love.

Sure, she could probably play John's game and simply go about her job as if nothing had ever happened between them. But unlike his, her heart was broken. There was no denying it any longer. The hurt Brian had caused her was nothing compared to working day in and day out with a man who'd been her lover.

So she knew what she must do: get another job, maybe at Lutheran Hospital, and put John Saville behind her. The way she felt about him, it would be the hardest thing she'd ever done. But as a nurse, she also knew that the best way to cure some hurts was to lance them quickly.

She was dismayed at how certain painful social moments were just that—over and gone in a blink, so far as time went. But when one had to relive them over and over in memory, the pain of it could endure a lifetime. Like overhearing a phone call or spotting the letter from Louise.

Tears filmed her eyes as she carried her clean laundry out to the Bronco. She chided herself for thinking again about just where John probably was this weekend: in the arms and bed of a woman she despised. The idea that he could be so cold and casual about sexual intimacy infuriated her and strengthened her resolve.

Yes, it would be hard to stick to her guns. No matter how much she denied it, John was not just one more bit player in the drama of her life—he was a fundamental part. For that very reason, she told herself, trying to feel determined and resolute, I've got to get another job.

Her cell phone chirred, and grateful for the distraction she pulled the phone out of her purse.

"Hello?"

"What's new, Boogaloo?" Hazel's throaty voice greeted her. "You busy right now?"

"Hi. Not really, I'm just driving home after a thrilling trip to the laundromat."

"Be out of your way to swing by? There's something I'd like to show you."

"I haven't passed your road yet, anyway. I'll be there in maybe five minutes."

"Good. Look for me out in the side yard."

"What's—"

But Hazel hung up before Rebecca could ask any questions.

She spotted Hazel in the big side yard even before she turned in at the stone gateposts of the Lazy M. The rancher was accompanied by a man Rebecca had glimpsed around town but never met. She parked behind a new pickup truck with huge toolboxes in the back and a yellow hard hat visible on the dashboard.

The doors of the truck advertised Dave Perry, Construction Contractor and included a phone number in nearby Lambertville. Now she guessed what was going on. Hazel had mentioned her intention to replace the old pump house, built in 1920, with a new one. Mountain snowmelt was low this year, and the Lazy M depended on pumps to keep water flowing to outlying irrigation ditches and stock ponds up in the summer pastures.

"Becky!" Hazel called to her as the latter threaded her way through the tall spruces toward them. "I'd like you to meet someone. Becky O'Reilly, this is Dave Perry."

He smiled at her from a face pleasantly tanned from years of outdoor work. He had a neat, closely trimmed beard slightly darker than the sandy-blond hair curling over the top of his collar. Dave Perry was lithe and slim-hipped, dressed in jeans and a clean flannel shirt, with a measuring tape clipped to one of his belt loops.

"Pleasure to meet you, Becky." The long, appreciative look he gave her showed that he was indeed pleased.

At the moment, however, male attention was not high on her lists of priorities.

"Dave stopped by to give me an estimate on a new pumping station," Hazel explained. "Naturally he wants to skin me alive on the price."

Dave glanced at Rebecca and sent her a quick wink to let her know he wasn't fooled by Hazel's tricks.

"She calls me the Robin Hood of construction contracting," he confided with another smile. "She claims I rob the rich and give to the poor—namely myself."

"Poor?" Hazel rolled her eyes. "What, is last year's hot tub out-of-date already?"

Despite her despondent mood, Rebecca had to smile at the pious, innocent face Dave assumed. Clearly he liked to clown around.

"Hazel, you've been fed vicious rumors about me. Why, I live so simply and humbly my neighbors call me the Dali Dave. And what *looks* like a satellite dish in my yard? It's really just a birdbath in the style of Picasso."

Both women laughed at Dave's charming silliness. By now, however, Rebecca fully realized he was the "something" Hazel wanted to show her. The incurable old romantic was up to her matchmaking tricks again, for it was in her nature to do her all for Mystery's future. "The quality of any town," she once insisted to Rebecca, "equals the quality of the people who live in it."

At the moment, however, Rebecca had little time to resent Hazel's meddling because she was forced to laugh repeatedly as the Matriarch of Mystery and Dali Dave concluded their business deal, drawing it out in true Western horse trader's fashion. Hazel complained bitterly that, land love us, she was a helpless old widow being fleeced. Dave stubbornly insisted he was practically giving the work away for nothing, for crying out loud. They eventually settled on the price they each knew beforehand would be agreed to. But this way was more fun.

Dave's truck was still meandering down the driveway when Hazel asked slyly, "Would *he* have been a better choice than Rick Collins?"

"I s'pose," Rebecca conceded without much interest.

"You 's'pose,'" Hazel exclaimed in disbelief. "Girl, I double-hog-tie dare you to look me in the eye and tell me you don't find Dave Perry attractive."

"Sure, he's all right," she conceded. "Lively sense of humor, too."

But something about the distracted, detached way she said it made Hazel study her for a moment, her eyes narrowing. "You know," she confessed, "I've got him in mind for your next date. Believe it or not, he's neither married nor gay, and he's definitely available. I noticed how he was checking you out nine ways to Sunday."

"No, thanks," Rebecca demurred. "Nothing against Dave. I'm sure plenty of women have their sights set on him."

"As a matter of fact, yep," Hazel affirmed, still watching her friend from shrewd eyes. "You *are* in love with John Saville, aren'cha?"

Rebecca flushed. That was answer enough for Hazel.

"Listen, hon," she urged Rebecca, "a date with a fun guy like Dave is just the tonic you need right now. Why become a she-hermit just because you've had some bad luck in love?"

However, Rebecca resolutely shook her head. She couldn't explain it to Hazel, but she simply could not "play the field" right now. Never mind that even as they spoke, John was probably with Louise, perhaps even making love to her. Until Rebecca managed to shake him out of her heart, she simply could not go out with another man.

"I'm going to be pretty busy for a while," she explained. "I'll be apartment hunting, and I may be looking for a new job, too."

"A new job? Becky, you're shooting a shotgun into a rain barrel. Just because you've had some little spat with John—"

"It's no spat," Rebecca said, her voice charged with feeling. "He isn't just an arrogant snob, Hazel. He's also a…well, he collects women in his bed, that's what. And I won't work for a man like him.''

"All right." Hazel surrendered. She knew Rebecca's moods to a hair—trying to change her mind, once it was set, was harder than holding the ocean back with a broom. "Well, if a handsome jasper like Dave Perry doesn't entice you, I'm out of options.''

"Are you *sure* about that?" Rebecca demanded. "The more I think about that date with Rick Collins, the more all the 'coincidences' bother me. Especially the fact that John showed up right on time to give me a ride home.''

"The Lord moves in mysterious ways," Hazel quoted, her face and tone exaggeratedly innocent.

"Yeah, well, so do you.''

Hazel shrugged. "Well, if a system works for the Lord…''

Unable to help herself, Rebecca laughed. "Hazel, shame on you! True, I didn't think much of Rick, but causing him all that trouble wasn't right.''

"Oh, pouf. Don't worry about that. I had one of my wranglers slip an envelope under his door anonymously. There was a hundred-dollar bill in it to compensate him for the trouble.''

Hazel's comment about being out of options may have seemed like surrender at last. But after Rebecca had left, Hazel remained out in the yard, turning this urgent problem back and forth for a while.

This is serious, she decided. Dave Perry had been the ace up her sleeve. Since the disaster-date plan had failed, she had decided to reverse her approach and set Rebecca up with a truly sexy, fun-filled guy—somebody to take her mind off John. But the poor girl was so far gone in love with her employer she was inconsolable.

This is a tough match, Hazel conceded again. She was still convinced, however, that Rebecca and John would be a superb couple if only the ''speed bumps'' on the road to love could be smoothed out. But Rebecca was on the verge of radical steps, such as quitting her job.

Hazel recalled that comment about how John Saville "collects women in his bed." She was convinced, despite a lack of any evidence, that Rebecca had him sized up all wrong. That young man was *not* a womanizer—he was steady and faithful, like an altar lamp that never goes out.

Her face settled into a mask of determination as she again stared toward the big main barn. The old foreman's quarters would need plenty of sprucing up, and quickly, but she had capable workers on her payroll. She must move swiftly now, or else this rocky *pas de deux* between John and Rebecca would soon be over.

"That's it," Dr. Saville finally announced, stepping back from the operating table and the heavily sedated young boy. He surveyed his work, peeling off his latex gloves. "Betcha fifty bucks this little guy won't even have a scar to prove we operated."

"Johnny, you wield a mean scalpel," praised Dr. Bob Morningstar. "They've come up with some impressive techniques for correcting hiatal hernias since I interned. I paid close attention to the way you tightened up that muscle wall without an incision. He won't even need any major painkillers after the anesthetic wears off."

"It's a piece of cake with a kid this young," John agreed. "But it gets more complicated to do as the patient ages."

The two men left surgery and peeled off their masks and scrubs, tossing them into a hamper.

"How 'bout a hot cuppa?" Bob suggested. The full-blooded Blackfoot Indian was about fifteen years older than his colleague, with thick salt-and-pepper hair, pronounced cheekbones and a strong, hawk nose. "Then you can come home with me, have a good dinner with the family. The kids have been asking about you."

"Sounds great."

Both doctors looked tired, for it was nearly 6:00 p.m., and they'd been performing surgeries at the Bitterroot Valley Indian Children's Hospital since 8:00 a.m.

"Another Saturday in the books," Bob remarked. "And you're scheduled for another full day tomorrow. I can't tell you how much we appreciate what you're doing, Johnny. It's hard as hell to lure surgeons out here to the boonies at mediocre pay. We're always shorthanded."

"Don't even bother to thank me," John assured him as both men headed toward the cafeteria for coffee. "Do you know how nice it is to have a place where I'm still 'Johnny?' Coming here is like coming home."

John didn't bother, however, to tell Bob another reason why he appreciated coming here on weekends. The hard concentration and long hours temporarily took his mind off Rebecca.

Life under a father who ran his home like a military boot camp had taught John to discipline everything except his emotions, which refused to be curbed by reason or even fatigue. All the hard work not only helped to keep his mind off Rebecca, it also kept him from dwelling on a cold, hard fact—he was that saddest of modern creatures, infinitely successful, yet infinitely lonely.

Coming to the Indian hospital to volunteer his badly needed services was the balm for his soul. The children he worked on were often abused and neglected, just as he had been; many of them came from dysfunctional families, just as he had. In a way that was very personal and private to him, each time he helped one of these innocent children, it helped to blot out the troubling memories. Nobody had been kinder to him, growing up, than his Native American neighbors—who had become more like family than neighbors.

Good family, not the kind he had.

"Something bothering you, Johnny?" Bob's voice cut into his musings over coffee. "You seem a little down in the dumps."

John mustered a weak smile. "Ahh—I've got a lady on my mind," he admitted. "Or actually, I'm trying to get her off my mind."

"That's paleface logic for you," Bob teased him fondly. "A young stag like you should have women on his mind plenty."

John laughed. But he couldn't hold the smile on his face—it slowly melted, replaced by a frown.

"Maybe some other woman," he replied. "But not this one."

"What, is she doing the hurt dance on you?"

"The thing is, I don't seem to have a snowball's chance in hell with her."

Bob snorted. "I find that hard to believe. Melt her heart, that's all it takes."

John set his cup down, startled. "What?"

"You heard me, melt her heart, man. Women can be very strong on the outside, even seem mean. But inside they are all soft places. Look at me—I'm homely as thirteen miles of bad road, and we both know it. But you've seen my wife. Is Sharon beautiful or not?"

"Absolutely beautiful," John said truthfully.

"Yeah, boy, it's that mix of Indian and Anglo blood, best of both. And you know how I hooked such a looker?"

"Speak, oh, wise one, I'm all ears."

"Not by sitting around glum-faced like you, that's for sure. I got to one of her soft places inside. See, three times I asked her out; three times she said no way. So then I sent her a little note: 'I have placed a stone in front of my house. When that stone melts, so too will my love for you.'"

"Smooth, lover boy."

"Well, anyhow it worked. That broke her inner resistance to me. Three days later she called me up and asked *me* out. The rest is matrimony, my friend. And that stone is still in front of our house.''

''Yeah, you're a natural-born poet. It's built into your language, but not in mine.''

''Into the heart, Johnny, the heart. Look, if this woman of yours is worth moping over, then go get her.''

John's pensive frown slowly transformed into a smile of admiration. Bob's advice echoed Hazel's, and maybe they were both right.

''Melt her heart, huh?'' he said thoughtfully.

Bob winked at his friend. ''You do that. The love of a good woman is priceless, my friend, the greatest treasure of them all.''

''I'll take your word for it,'' John assured him. ''But if it is a treasure, then so far I've misplaced the key.''

Thirteen

"**D**r. Saville? Have you got a moment?"

Rebecca's voice seemed to startle him back to reality. Although a medical journal lay open before him on the desk, his attention had long since wandered outside to the tree-lined streets of Mystery. Not yet 9:00 a.m., but Monday was already shaping up as a beautiful, sun-drenched day. Outside, at least, he thought as he took in her stern, purposeful features.

He rose quickly, watching her. "Of course, Becky. Have a seat."

Now I'm Becky again, she told herself. But on Friday I was Miss O'Reilly. Maybe his "therapeutic weekend" has left him in a laid-back mood. Obviously, judging from the shadows under his eyes, he didn't set any records for sleeping.

The chair in front of his desk seemed too close for comfort, so she perched on the edge of the sofa, and he sank back into his soft leather desk chair.

"What's on your mind?" he added.

Something's different about him, she thought with some confusion. Not just calling me Becky—the rigid, imperious manner of last Friday was gone.

But don't be distracted from your task. Don't start making excuses, she lectured herself.

"This isn't my two-week notice or anything," she informed him, speaking a bit too quickly. "But I know it takes time to find nurses, so I wanted to let you know early that I'm looking for another job. That way you'll have time to replace me."

"Replace you?" he repeated with some confusion, as if not quite understanding English. "You mean you're quitting?"

His attitude of confused betrayal irritated her. He of all people had no right to make her feel guilty.

"As I just said," she repeated in an impatient tone, "I'm looking for another job. Obviously, that means I'd have to quit this job to take another."

He frowned slightly.

"I'm interviewing next week at Lutheran Hospital. They need surgical-recovery nurses. I know the shift supervisor, Amy Jackman. She taught my anatomy class in nursing school, and...she's been...been encouraging me to apply."

It became increasingly more difficult to organize and complete her thoughts. How could she when his eyes were so obviously pained.

"They'll snap you right up," John said stiffly. "You easily have the skills and knowledge of a nurse with ten years' more experience."

"Thank you."

"Is it—I mean, is it money?" he demanded. "If the raise I gave you wasn't—"

"It's not the money," she assured him. "I'll be making almost the same salary if I'm hired at Lutheran."

Their eyes met, held, and Rebecca saw his conflicting emotions like miniature storms raging in his eyes.

"Then is it the situation between us?" he asked frankly.

"No."

"Sure it is. What else could it be?"

"It's…it's *me*. Not you, not us, it's me."

"How do you mean?" he demanded.

"What we did at my place. It was a mistake."

"I thought you said you don't regret what we did."

It took an effort to hold her own contradictory emotions in check. "I did say that, and I still mean it. What I really regret is all that has happened afterward."

It was a lame, unclear remark, and she knew it. She had *meant* to bring up the subject of his "recreational weekends," but she couldn't quite bring herself to be that specific—or presumptuous.

"Afterward?" he repeated, his tone mocking the word. "Correct me if I'm wrong, but nothing much at all has happened. Between us, I mean. I tried to ask you out, is all, and you shot me right down." He boldly accused her with his eyes.

"You didn't exactly ask me out," she said, soldiering on bravely. "You attempted to squeeze me in on a week night schedule, remember? So you could leave your weekends free."

"Oh, well, pardon me all to hell," he flung at her in exasperation, "for not supplying you with my complete monthly itinerary before we made love. Maybe you should print up a questionnaire to make sure we men will be acceptable to your timetable."

At these cutting words, her defiant frown became a mask of angry contempt. "*You* should talk about a questionnaire. Believe me, I've had my fingers crossed since having unprotected sex with *you*. And I don't mean pregnancy, either."

Both of them had raised their voices as their altercation
escalated. Now, at the worst possible moment, Lois poked
her head into the office.

"Dr. Saville? Becky?" she reproved the two of them
with her tone. "Wendy Johnson is here for her appointment."

Rebecca flushed deeply, realizing Lois, at least, had
heard that "fingers crossed" comment. Perhaps even
Wendy had.

"Of course, Lois," she managed calmly even though her
pulse still throbbed hard in that temple vein of hers. "I'm
on my way."

She left the office without even looking at John again.

He called up the main menu on his computer screen and
selected Wendy Johnson's patient file, beginning to review
it. But angry frustration directed at Becky kept intruding
into his thoughts.

He was trying, damn it all, to follow Bob Morningstar's
and Hazel's advice. But it was virtually impossible to melt
a woman's heart while she was insulting him—reminding
him how much she regretted ever making love with him,
at that.

If this woman is worth having, Bob's voice echoed in
memory, *then quit moping and go get her.*

Open up a little, Hazel's mellow, throaty voice goaded
him. *Be patient with Becky.*

Yeah, right, he thought bitterly as he grabbed his stethoscope off the corner of the desk and rose to go see his
patient. Any opening he gave Rebecca was just one more
spot where she could stick the knife in.

"This is one marriage I just might not be able to pull
off," Hazel confided to Lois early on Tuesday evening.
"The unstoppable force, I'm afraid, has met the immovable
object. But I'm giving it one more try. Once those two

stubborn fools get their pride out of the way, they'll be abl
to see what a fine couple they make.''

The two women stood in the main room of the forme
quarters once occupied by the foreman of the Lazy M. *
few years ago a brand-new bunkhouse had been built, com
plete with new quarters for the foreman. Since then th
four-room apartment in the main barn had stood deserted

''You're absolutely right that they'll be stuck with eacl
other,'' Lois conceded, glancing around the small quarters
''Once you manage to get them back here. No windows
and only the one door leading in off the tack room. Bu
it's going to be a tricky piece of work getting them botl
back here at exactly the same time.''

A crafty glint sparkled in Hazel's eyes.

''Oh, it's going to take some fine acting on my part,'
she admitted. ''Especially since I'll be faking illness to foo
a sharp doctor and nurse. You're right about the timing
too. Fortunately, I can push both of those youngsters aroun
a little. Age has its perks. Russ?''

A young cowboy, who was busy stocking a small refrig
erator with food and beverages, glanced up from his task
He was the same lad who had put Rick Collins's truck ou
of commission by deflating one of its giant tires.

''Yeah, boss?''

''Remember, you'll need to be well hidden in the tacl
room. And you'll need to *stay* hidden until they both com
inside.''

He grinned. Like Hazel, he was clearly enjoying all thi:
hugger-mugger, which was why she always picked him fo
any task requiring trickery and deceptions. To him this wa:
all like practical jokes, and she'd never met a cowboy ye
who didn't relish a good practical joke.

''No sweat, boss woman,'' he assured her. ''You luri
'em out here, and I'll spring the chute on 'em.''

Even now two more hands were hard at work, sprucin{

up the old quarters. The rooms had been thoroughly cleaned, the refrigerator and cupboards well stocked. Hazel's housekeeper had already stocked the bathroom linen closet and made up the bed.

"We'll be making our play on Thursday afternoon," Hazel told Russ. "That's perfect because Lois tells me the medical suite will be closed all day Friday for painting. That means it'll be a three-day weekend."

"You can't keep them prisoners for three days!" Lois exclaimed.

Hazel laughed. "Oh, I know that. We'll spring 'em sometime the next day."

"Becky may be awfully mad," Lois cautioned.

"I can wrangle Becky," Hazel scoffed. She cast another glance around the rustic apartment. "Not exactly the Waldorf, is it? There's no whirlpool in the bathroom, that's for sure. Not even a tub, just a shower. But all the plumbing works."

"Pretty basic," Lois agreed. "But it's comfy and clean. Private, too."

Hazel patted a solid old armchair in the living room. "Personally, I can't stand these sissy living rooms with swags of drapery everywhere and all those fussy little cushions every place you want to sit. And furniture that breaks at the first rough use it gets. *This* place is solid as bedrock."

She paused, thinking about the news that had brought Lois by.

"So Becky wants a new job?" she mused aloud. "I knew she was looking to move, but this sounds like a complete makeover of her life. Listen—has she said anything to you about what happened between them after the bus accident? You know, on that day they both took off from work?"

Lois shook her head. "Not in so many words. Becky's

a pretty private person when it comes to stuff like that. But isn't it obvious what must have happened?''

Russ was out of hearing range now. ''Part of it is,'' Hazel replied. ''Those two slept together, all right. And they both liked it just fine. Mutual attraction is not their problem.''

''No,'' Lois agreed. ''They're plenty hot for each other. Their main problem is John's lost weekends. I can tell you right now, Hazel—it won't matter how much Becky loves him. If John *is* having an affair, with Louise Wallant or any other woman, Becky will not forgive him.''

''Nor should she,'' Hazel agreed. ''The whole point of being in love is to feel special in the eyes of the person you love. Being a name on a list—even if it's a short list— is hardly special.''

''Do you think he's having an affair?''

Hazel shook her head. ''I don't. I think Becky is the only filly he wants in his stable. That young man is a true-blue romantic, just like Becky.''

''Then why,'' Lois asked, ''is he being so secretive about where he goes on the weekends?''

''Dogged if I know, hon.''

Hazel took another look around the nearly ready apartment. ''That's why we're pulling off this little deception. If we can just trap those two together long enough, they'll *have* to open up to each other.''

Russ, who overheard this last remark, looked up from his task to grin wickedly at his boss. He showed her the bottle of champagne he was about to put in the fridge.

''Either that,'' he reminded her, ''or they'll tear into each other like two badgers in a barrel.''

Fourteen

The work week, it seemed to Rebecca, passed with agonizing slowness. The hours after work, most of which she spent apartment hunting, fairly flew by, for they kept her thoughts elsewhere. But time spent at the medical suite dragged by like rainy days. Constant proximity to John was unavoidable, and the contrast between now and the times they'd briefly gotten along made her heart ache over the broken promise of their love.

Recovering from his initial disappointment that she was quitting, John began searching for her replacement with a seeming vengeance. He called the county's only employment office, and by Thursday he'd already interviewed the first two applicants. One of whom looked like a professional beauty-contest winner.

No surprise, Rebecca fumed silently, that the attractive, leggy one received a much longer interview.

"Am I glad the office is closed tomorrow," she told Lois

near the end of Thursday afternoon. "Three whole days away from hi—from this place. The sooner I get another job, the happier I'll be. The only thing I'm gonna miss around here is you, Lo."

"So I'm a 'thing' now?"

"Oh, you know what I mean."

"Mmm-hmm," Lois responded, "I know *who* you mean, sure."

Rebecca could have sworn a knowing smile flickered in her friend's eyes for a moment. "What?" she demanded. For several days now Lois had been acting as if she knew a secret and had no plans to share it. "Why that smug tone?"

"Oh, stop being so paranoid," Lo rebuked her. "It's just you two, you and John—if it wasn't such a shame what you're doing, it would be comical."

Their employer was back in his office with Doug Ott, the day's last patient, for a consultation. Rebecca bridled at her friend's comment. "What are you babbling about?" she demanded. "*What's* a shame?"

"Yeah, right, like you don't know. I'm not babbling, have eyes to see, ears to hear. All week long it's been 'Dr Saville, this' and 'Miss O'Reilly, that,' you two all stilted and formal. Each of you like cocked weapons with hair triggers, close to exploding. When in truth both of you would rather channel all that energy in bed with each other."

Rebecca's nostrils flared in sudden anger. "I realize there's a long, long list of women praying for that privilege," she returned sarcastically. "But my name's not on it."

She deeply regretted that last sentence when Lois suddenly laughed and said, "Anymore."

Rebecca flushed and turned back to her computer, but Lois wasn't fooled for a moment. Keeping her voice down she chanted a little jump-rope rhyme to the tune of "Reuben, Reuben, I've Been Thinking":

"Sy and I went to the cir-cus,
Sy got hit with a rolling pin;
We got even with the cir-cus,
We bought tickets but we didn't go in!"

"That's you and John," Lois explained. "You both got hurt a little. Now you think you can get even by denying what you both really want most. All you're doing is punishing yourselves. Like two little kids mad at the circus."

Despite her anger, Rebecca was shaken up by Lois's quiet, thoughtful insight.

Lois read those feelings in her face and smiled. "I'm pulling rank on you, babe, that's all. Believe me, when you make twenty years of marriage actually work, it teaches you some psychology."

Before Rebecca could say anything, however, John and Doug emerged from his office, still quietly talking, and came up front to the reception area.

While Doug and Lois settled his account, John stopped at Rebecca's desk. "Miss O'Reilly, before you leave today would you kindly pull the Conroy X-rays from the files and leave them on my door? I requested them this morning."

His indignant tone seemed far more resentful than the trivial matter justified.

"The X-rays have been on your door for hours, Doctor," she replied with icy precision. "Go check the envelope."

"Oh, well..." He looked a little nonplussed. But his tone remained resentful. "Anyone can make a simple mistake."

He hesitated, then decided to add one more thing.

Suddenly Rebecca understood the real reason for his ticked-off tone.

"And by the way, it was rude and unprofessional of you

to decline a meeting with Shannon when she interviewed. She asked about your duties, and I hoped you would fill her in. You said you wanted to help with the transition.''

Oh, it's 'Shannon' already, she thought. Did he actually interview her, or did he just stare at her body and dispense the laid-back, sexy charm he reserved for women in fox stoles and luxury cars?

After all, though a knockout, Shannon wasn't wealthy.

"I didn't exactly refuse," she fibbed. "I had a patient on the phone when you called me. By the time I got off, she was leaving.''

"You deliberately *kept* that patient on the line until Shannon left," he challenged.

"Yeah? Well, too bad for Miss Perky," she retorted. "I've got the feeling she's already hired, anyway, I must be a psychic or something.''

"Something," he agreed grimly just before slamming his door.

"Oh, my, my," Lois said, the last patient gone now. She shook her neat blond head in amazement. "Gonna punish that old circus," she teased.

"Circus schmircus," Rebecca snapped, still miffed. As if all that mattered were Shannon's injured sensibilities. "The man's not only arrogant and conceited, he's shallow. And he talks about rude? 'I requested them this morning.' Well he can just bully someone else, because soon he won't have me to push around. I just hope he doesn't turn on you, Lois.''

"God forbid," Lois agreed, barely keeping a straight face.

Despite her brave and determined words, Rebecca gave vent to her turbulent emotions during the drive back to her apartment. As hot tears spilled over her lashes, she berated herself again for the moment of sexual surrender with John. It had been so wonderful while they made love—a pleasure and oneness she'd never in her life experienced. It could not have been better. But the pain and anger she'd felt since then, the humiliation at the way he treated her, as if she were trying to guilt-trip him or somehow sink her hooks into him.

And this jealousy she felt—this nagging worry about Louise or whoever was sharing his mystery weekends with him. She hated all of it, and she *must* endure the pain of leaving his life for good. Otherwise it would just get worse.

She cheered herself up somewhat with the reminder that tomorrow she might select her new place. She'd found a cedar town house in Lambertville that was in her price range, and she had an appointment to see it this very evening. If she landed a job at Lutheran Hospital, which seemed a done deal already, she'd be only five minutes drive from work—and would rarely ever see John, who did most of his surgery at Valley General.

She took a quick shower, then changed into black leather pumps and a plum V-neck dress with a wide, flowing skirt. She was still combing out her wet hair when the telephone chirred.

Caller ID showed it was Hazel's number, so she picked up. "Hi, Hazel."

"Hey, hon. Got big plans for this weekend?"

"Don't I wish," Rebecca muttered, though she was instantly wary of Hazel's tricks. "Why—what's up?"

"Mainly I'm just wondering if you'd agree to spend the weekend with me at the Lazy M?"

The request was oddly worded, and Rebecca wasn't sure where it was headed. "Wait a minute, Hazel. Is this another setup for a date?"

"Actually, I'm not quite up to that stuff," Hazel assured her. "The thing is, I'm a mite off my feed, Becky. I feel tired and a little achy."

"Has Donna taken your temperature?"

"Yes, and it's just a little high. Almost a hundred."

Not serious, Rebecca thought, but often a slight elevation signaled that the body's immune system was kicking in.

"Could be you're fighting off a bug," she suggested lightly.

Although she kept her voice calm, Rebecca felt a little prickle of alarm. It wasn't Hazel's temperature that worried her—it was her weary tone. It didn't signal an emergency, perhaps, but given Hazel's lifelong energy and her "keep up the strut" McCallum confidence, this defeated, vulnerable tone was worrisome.

Without a second thought, she decided to call and reschedule her appointment to see the town house.

"It would be fun to spend the weekend," she told Hazel, eager to help the woman who had done so much for her. "How 'bout I toss a few things into a bag and come right on over?"

"I do appreciate it, sweet love. Donna's making her delicious chicken Kiev, we'll have a nice dinner. Maybe you could do some riding while you're here. That three-year-old ginger you like so much needs to shake out the kinks."

"Well your temperature is perfect," John told Hazel, reading a digital thermometer in the soft light of a bedside lamp. "Ninety-eight point six precisely. And your blood pressure and pulse are normal, too."

He took a small penlight from his kit and examined each of her eyes.

"It was awfully sweet of you to come over like this, John," Hazel assured him as he peered into each cornea. "It just came on so suddenly, I—well, maybe I sort of overreacted."

"Nonsense," he assured her. "I'm happy to come check on any neighbor, but especially you. Stick out your tongue and say ahh...that's it, good."

He switched off his light, dropped the used tongue depressor into a nearby waste can, and announced, "Hazel, if you were any fitter, I'd put you on the Olympic team."

Although still respectful, there was suspicion in his tone. She aimed a covert glance at the clock on the nightstand. If Rebecca arrived when she'd promised to, the timing should be just right.

"Now, now, Doctor, you know how it is with us seasoned citizens—better safe than sorry."

"Hmm...what, exactly, did you say you felt?"

"It was sort of like a twitching sensation in my chest."

"A twitching?"

She shook her head. "No, maybe it was more like a fluttering."

John grinned briefly. "Perhaps we should consult the dictionary to see which you felt?"

"I'll go with fluttering," Hazel decided as if picking an entrée.

"Any dizziness in the past few days?"

"Possibly," Hazel said, hedging, and John's eyes narrowed.

"Possibly?" he repeated. "You're not sure?"

"Well, the thing of it is, I haven't fainted," she clarified, her face focused as if trying to remember. "But there *may* have been a brief dizzy spell."

John definitely didn't trust her. She was acting a little too innocent, a little too confused and hesitant. That was nothing like the Hazel McCallum he knew.

"Have you had a recurrence of your angina pains?" he asked next.

Hazel was about to respond when a two-tone chime out in the living room announced the arrival of a visitor.

"Donna will get it," she remarked.

He aimed a stern, yet curious, glance at her. "Hazel, you're faking this illness, aren't you?"

While she was a gifted actress, when the cause of love required it, Hazel had never been a very good liar when directly confronted. Now, hearing voices approach the bedroom, she quickly resorted to another tack.

"Yes, I'm faking," she admitted. The ailing tone was gone. "You thick-skulled, high-strung youngsters have forced me to it. And now you're going to play along."

"Hazel, I can't—"

"Shush it! She's almost here. Do you want Becky or not?"

"Becky? But how does she—"

He never finished the question, for at that very moment the lady in question appeared in the bedroom door, carrying a nylon overnight bag and a leather jumpkit similar to John's.

"Hazel, what—" She paused in midsentence when she saw him standing beside the bed. For a few moments her face closed in anger against him. But then she saw his open bag and the stethoscope around her neck. Worry suddenly replaced her anger.

"I called John right after I talked to you, hon," Hazel explained, the under-the-weather tone back in her voice. "I felt a little twinge. John thinks it might be my angina kicking up."

"Oh." Rebecca looked uncertainly from one to the other. John seemed on the verge of saying something. But his eyes took in all of Rebecca, from her well-turned ankles to those lovely arching eyebrows, and the faintest of smiles lifted one corner of his mouth. He remained silent.

"Have you taken your nitro?" she asked Hazel.

"I was just telling John," the matriarch spoke up quickly, "that Donna has looked all over the goldang house for them. I seem to've misplaced them."

"If John writes a prescription," Rebecca offered, "I can run into town quick and—"

"Oh, I know where I left them," Hazel cut in suddenly. "I've been working on the old foreman's quarters out in the barn. I had them out there with me and must have left them there."

"Where? I'll run out and get them," Rebecca volunteered.

Hazel's weather-seamed face tightened in a show of concentration. "Let me see…did I leave them on the kitchen counter? Or maybe it was on the stand beside the sofa…oh, botheration, I can't recall."

"I'll go out there and look," Rebecca said, starting to turn away. "You go through the tack room, right?"

"That's right, Becky, the door should be unlocked."

John was still standing beside the bed, gazing at Rebecca. Hazel quickly reached out and gave him a little punch on the arm to goad him into action.

"A backbone," she whispered as the younger woman left the bedroom, "not a wishbone, remember?"

He snapped quickly into action. "Just a second, Becky," he called behind his departing nurse. "I'll help you look."

The moment he, too, had left the bedroom Hazel sat up in bed and pulled a wireless phone out from under the covers. She quickly tapped in a number.

"Get your rear in gear, Russ," she ordered the hidden cowboy in the barn. "They're on their way out."

Fifteen

John caught up with Rebecca even before she left the house. It was apparent to him that her concerns about her friend's health outweighed any suspicions she had of Hazel's motives.

"What is it, John?" she asked the moment they left the house. "Her heart?"

"If so, it's nothing I can tell without an EKG," he replied, promising himself he would tell no lies even though Hazel was deceiving them. "Her heartbeat is regular and strong, and her blood pressure is 130 over 80."

"Well...did she describe her symptoms to you?"

He recalled Hazel's evasive talk of "flutters" and "twitches." It was hard to keep a straight face when he replied. "Not too clearly."

Rebecca sent him a quizzical glance. "Does she still have a slight fever?"

"No fever at all."

"No fever?" They were halfway to the barn now, twilight gathering around them. "But she told me her temp was up slightly."

"Maybe it was, but it's fine now."

"I wonder," she mused, more to herself than John. Hazel's phone call had left her with stretched nerves. If it turned out she was playing another one of her little matchmaking games, Rebecca was going to read her the riot act.

They reached the cavernous main barn, and she flipped the toggle, opening the sliding doors. Overhead lights winked on automatically. She shivered slightly as a chilly breeze whispered around them, suddenly very aware of John's nearness.

"The tack room's toward the back," she told him as they moved inside. "The living quarters Hazel mentioned are used as a storage room now. We'll have to go through the tack room to reach it."

"You know plenty about the ranch, don't you?" he remarked as they strolled through the long barn. Cows of various breeds watched them from placid eyes.

"I could run the place," she admitted. "The Lazy M was my second home. Especially after my mom died and with my dad gone so much."

"Yeah, I can relate to that," he assured her. "I spent a lot of my childhood on the Blackfoot Indian reservation."

"You did?" His remark genuinely surprised her, for it did not fit her preconceived ideas about his youth.

But before she could ask him about it, they'd reached the tack room. The familiar, pleasant smell of leather, saddle soap and horse liniment reminded her she'd been away too long from this life. She pointed to a closed door midway in the rear wall.

"That's the entrance to the foreman's quarters. I hope Hazel left it unlocked."

The door opened when she turned the knob. She flipped

the wall switch, and light flooded the interior. They both stepped inside. This first room was the kitchen, brightly painted and cozy.

"What in the world?" she wondered aloud, startled at what she saw.

"This place is hardly a storage room," John pointed out, looking all around them. "It's neat as a pin. Is someone still living here, you think? Anybody home?" he added, raising his voice.

No answer from within. There was no sign of dust or cobwebs, either, and the entire apartment had a fresh, clean-scrubbed smell. The old but serviceable appliances gleamed.

"If it's not used any longer," John said, "why is the refrigerator plugged in and humming?"

They moved into a small dining room off the kitchen. Both of them gaped in astonishment when they saw a two-branched gilt candlestick on the small gateleg table—candles already lit.

"This is kind of spooky," he remarked. "Those candles have hardly burned. Somebody must have lit them in the past few minutes."

"*Spooky* isn't quite the right word," she countered as it began to sink in what Hazel was pulling off here.

Lit candles weren't the half of it. A small wooden tub on a nearby sideboard was filled with ice, barely beginning to melt, and a magnum of champagne. An oval wicker basket on the table held bunches of fragrant red and white carnations. Becky read the card beside them, written in Hazel's distinctive hand: "For the flower girl."

Her eyes met John's. She felt suddenly defensive, afraid he'd think *she* was part of this deception. "We've been had by a mastermind."

He nodded, an amused smile replacing his baffled look. "Look—the table's even set for us. You ever get the feeling, around Hazel, that you're just a chess piece being moved around?''

"Do I ever. But it's *not* going to work," she vowed, turning to leave. "Hazel presumes too much on her white hairs. This time she's gone too far. Well, she can cry wolf about being sick. But she can't make me stay here if I don't want to.''

"Hey, where you going?"

"Where do you think? I'm going to march right back to the house and give her a piece of my mi—''

She abruptly fell silent when, halfway back into the kitchen, she spotted the closed door.

"Did you shut that?'' she demanded of John.

"No. And spare me that dirty look, *I'm* not playing any tricks on you. Maybe the door just swung shut behind us.''

Rebecca then discovered, with a sinking feeling, that the thick, solid wood door refused to budge.

His denial just now struck her as sounding a little staged. She whirled around, glowering at him as her suspicions suddenly widened. "*Did* the two of you plan all this?''

Angry resentment hardened his handsome features. "There you go again, giving vent to your unlimited ego. I'm not so desperate for female companionship that I need to trap women in barns.''

"*My* unlimited ego? Don't make me laugh. I'm not the one who needs to carve notches on my bedpost to 'validate' myself.''

"Just what the hell does that mean?''

"Did you and Hazel cook this up?''

"I told you no. So get over it, okay? I was sucked in just like you were. I admit I guessed, just before you arrived, that Hazel was faking the illness, all right? But I did *not* know about any of this.''

Rebecca believed him, but in her irritation she didn't

care. She pounded on the door, her fist making pitifully little sound on the thick heart pine.

"Help!" she cried out. "Help, somebody! We're locked in."

"I'll try the phone," John suggested, seeing one on the wall near the door.

Not surprisingly, though, it was dead.

"Is there another door?" he demanded.

She shook her head in helpless frustration. "No windows, either, since it's all an interior apartment. The place has ventillation shafts for fresh air, but they're too small for a person to fit in them."

"That lock should be pretty old," he reasoned. "Got a bobby pin?"

She slid one from her hair, and he bent it open, then knelt before the door and began working on the lock. However, after about fifteen minutes with no luck, he gave up.

"Well then, we might as well face it," he told her, his own voice resigned. "Hazel didn't go to all this trouble just to lock us up for a few minutes. We won't get out until she *wants* us out. So why injure your hand beating on the door? We might as well make the best of it."

"Meaning what?" she demanded.

He shrugged, heading toward the refrigerator. "Suit yourself. I'm hungry. I'm going to see what our captor has given us for supper."

"I can take an informed guess," she predicted sarcastically as he opened the refrigerator. "Chicken Kiev in a casserole dish, ready for warming in the oven. With a little note from Donna taped to it—twenty minutes at 325 degrees."

He glanced inside, eyes widening in surprise when he spotted the casserole dishes, three of them, with the very note taped to one.

"Sounds like you know the drill around here, all right,"

he speculated quietly, watching her with eyes narrowing. "Besides the chicken Kiev, there are steamed asparagus tips and boiled new potatos. You *sure* you're not in cahoots with Hazel?"

"Why not?" she riposted, her tone rising in anger. "We gold diggers and guilt trippers will stop at nothing to trap our prey."

"I didn't go *that* far," he taunted, as if enjoying her little tantrum. "But I'm glad you thought to include fresh eggs—for breakfast."

The hit scored, and his sudden laughter left her speechless with indignation.

How dare he assume she would stoop to…to…

But she lost the thought as renewed anger at Hazel surged into her thoughts again. Rebecca had forgiven her for other unwelcome intrusions and trickery; this, however, was simply outrageous. Hazel had gone over the line this time, and she needed to be told that.

"She played on our concern for her," she fumed. "When all along she was just luring us in like…like bugs to a zap light."

He laughed at her comparison as he popped the casserole into the small electric oven and set the temperature.

"You should preheat the oven," she remarked absently.

"Bachelor doesn't mean stupid," he teased. "I set the timer for an extra few minutes. Is it really that bad?" he added.

"What?"

"Having to be here with me?"

He turned from the stove and crossed his arms over his chest, watching her with a sexy, sly smile that stirred heat and desire within her. He wore a short-sleeved khaki shirt, and she admired his muscular forearms and the fine, dark-brown hairs covering them.

Even as she felt her ardent, needful response to him,

however, she reminded herself how ideal this situation was for him. He could have a little fun until Hazel sprang them loose, then wave bye-bye and head to Deer Lodge.

She had no desire whatsoever to accuse him of anything, only to ignore him as best she could.

So her next outburst surprised her as much as him.

"I guess you wouldn't mind a little spur of the moment trysting." The words sprang out of her. "I won't be keeping you from Louise, will I, or any of your more deserving and qualified lovers?"

"Louise?" he repeated uncertainly. "Man, you just lost me on that one."

Horrified at her outburst, she had determined to just shut up. But she could not remain silent.

"You know good and well I mean Louise Wallant," she said softly.

Recognition dawned. The expression on his face set. "Look, Louise and I are friends, sure. We know each other from way back. That's no illicit secret."

"No, maybe not. But where you spend every other weekend seems to be a secret. It's only logical that you've been spending it with her." Rebecca's heart was numb. She slowly lowered herself to a chair. "Look, Louise Wallant and you really don't concern me. It's none of my business. It's just—just—well, things got out of hand between us that one time. We did things we shouldn't have. I see now I want more from a man than a couple of dates whenever he's decided to stay in town for the weekend."

"I don't spend every other weekend at Deer Lodge with Louise Wallant, if that's what this is about."

He didn't seem to be lying, she realized, despite her growing confusion. He was too sincere, and besides, lies would be too easy to expose. All she had to do is ask Louise.

"But you said you had specific reasons for coming to

Mystery, for settling here," she reminded him. Looking away, she added, "I figured it was a woman."

"It's not a woman. Not yet, anyway," he added cryptically. "I came here because it was the nearest place to the Bitterroot Valley that needed a surgeon. I wanted to be close enough so that I could drive to Bitterroot Valley on weekends."

He took her arm and drew her up from the chair. Slowly his arms encircled her. "I'm not having an affair with anyone, Becky. I volunteer my time at the children's hospital on the reservation. They have no funds for extra surgeons but plenty of need."

"That's something to be proud of.... Why in the world would you keep it a secret?"

This time his smile was a little more wistful. "The heart is a lonely hunter, remember?"

He stared hard at her for a long time, as if trying to assess whether he could trust her or not.

Finally, when he seemed to have made up his mind, he said, "I know this might sound dumb to others. But I didn't want anyone to know because one of the reasons I do it is that my own family was so dirt poor and dysfunctional. I'm not whining when I tell you this, just being honest. My dad was a broken-down failure who abused the hell out of me, my mother and his liver—alcohol killed him."

His frank, calm tone made it clear he didn't want pity, he wanted just to get it off his chest. "The Indian families near me sort of adopted me, just the way Hazel adopted you—not in court, maybe, but in everyday fact. No matter how many times my old man booted me out in a drunken rage, I never wanted for a place to sleep or a hot meal. Now I just want to give back something to them for all they gave me, you know what I mean? I just don't talk about it because to explain my deep relationship to the reservation requires me to explain my relationship with my father—and I'm sure as hell not proud of that.''

She stared up at him, not sure, not yet willing to hope. ''Okay, that explains what you do with your time. It doesn't explain how cold you've been to me when every socialite in town purrs on your arm.''

He laughed so hard he almost roared. ''That's a great observation, Becky, and it's true. I can make those kind of women purr. I know them so well. What surgeon doesn't? All you have to do to make those kind happy is give them a costly trinket and a designer handbag. They're no mystery at all. They don't confound me.''

He wrapped her in his arms and looked down at her. ''But then there's Rebecca, with the wild untamed hair and spirit to match. You're nothing but a mystery to me, and if I've come off cold, it's just that I've found myself out of my element with you. I don't know what will make you happy, or if I'm the guy to do it.''

She stared up at him, noting the love in his voice for his friends, the intensity of his features as he talked about deeply personal feelings. Only a strong and good man, she thought, could have overcome that background to become what and who he is today.

A tight bubble of emotion swelled within her chest, and she hardly trusted her voice. ''I'm no mystery, Dr. Saville. I just want love and commitment and a family.''

It all suddenly overwhelmed her—the full realization of how wrong she had been about him, how unfair. Her own insecurities had somehow taken hold of her and crushed her good sense. Now she looked like a fool. A jealous, vulnerable fool.

His knuckles brushed along the smooth line of her cheek. In a voice rough with meaning, he said, ''If you need to know anything about me, *anything*,'' he emphasized, ''all you have to do is ask. I believe in honesty in relationships.''

She closed her eyes, sick with regret. "Sometimes asking is the hardest thing in the world to do. Especially if you're terrified of the answers."

Her eyes opened. She knew tears glistened in them, but she had no more walls to put up. Now was the time to bare all. And pray there would be pieces left of her heart to pick up afterward.

Staring up at him, she confessed, "I didn't think we had a relationship. I suppose that's why I've been so cold. You were going off on your mysterious weekends, and I knew that day we spent together could very easily have been chalked up to just one of those things—especially for a big time bachelor M.D. But I couldn't keep you from affecting me. I guess I just couldn't relinquish the hope and need for something more between us. I just couldn't relinquish it," she finished with a whisper.

"But why should you? I became a doctor because I care about people, Rebecca. I'm not the kind of guy who wants one-night stands and throw-away girlfriends." His embrace grew tighter, his expression more intense. "Look, I was afraid to be too pushy. I knew that one time between us took us both by surprise. But I also knew I wanted more. And not just more sex, more *you*. But you were skittish, so I just figured it was me. That I was too uptight, too con-trolled for you—"

"It wasn't you. It's never been you," she blurted out, wiping the tears from her cheek. "It was me, okay? I just didn't want another doctor to pass me up for a better class of woman." She tried to pull away, but his hands became manacles, refusing her escape.

She shook her head, trying to entice him to let her go, but he wouldn't. Finally her body went limp against his. The tears came fast now.

"I was jilted by another doctor," she said, the words bitter on her tongue. "I fancied myself pretty much in love

with the guy. Imagine my surprise when he told me my
community college background wasn't going to quite cut it
on the way up the ladder to his success. He left me for a
woman who already had everything—a woman very much
like Louise Wallant. And there I was, little old Rebecca
O'Reilly, holding the empty bag again. I just—just wanted
to forgo a repeat experience. Once was enough in my life,
thank you. And besides—''

She swallowed and finally stared him in the eye. ''Besides, what I felt for Brian was nothing compared to how
I feel for you. I didn't think I could ever stand your rejection, and so the best way to protect myself was to not get
involved.''

He drew her even closer. His arms locked around her
shoulders. His mouth kissed away the tears. Nuzzling her
hair, he said nothing for long sweet moments. Finally, in a
lover's whisper, he said, ''Becky, you are who you are
because you're involved. That's so much of your beauty.
Don't withhold it.''

She wanted to shout with joy. All the emotion she'd
longed to show him seemed to demand release all at once.
But once in freefall, the unknown assailed her. Her heart
was captured, no doubt about it. But the ending was still
unclear.

The timer on the oven dinged. The mood shifted.

''Dinner's ready,'' he announced, holding her eyes with
his. ''Shall we delay it?''

''Let's.''

He pulled her against his chest; she surrendered to the
strength of his arms. His lips found hers, warm and pliant
and electrifying, and the hunger that drove them had nothing to do with dinner.

She pulled away first, breathless. ''I think it's safe to say
we have all night.''

He smiled and kissed her eyes shut. ''Yeah, twelve glo-
rious hours. Let's take our time. You can yell at Hazel all
you want to. I think she's one cool gal.''

Sixteen

"You've taken plenty of blame for the misunderstandings between us," John remarked over dinner in the cozy, candlelit dining room. "But a lot of the problems between us were my fault, too. I remained silent too often, and that created wrong impressions."

"Why? Was it just your background?" Rebecca pressed him.

"Fear of failure. I see that now."

"Fear of failure? You, a sought-after surgeon who publishes several articles a year in top medical journals?"

His smile was self-deprecating. "Weird, huh? But I've found out the hard way—early brainwashing goes down deep inside your genes. My dad was always screaming at me, 'Failure is *not* an option.' I realized long ago he knew nothing about life skills. But no matter how much I really wanted to open up to you, I had this...I don't know, visceral fear of rejection. All stemming from the old days at home."

He reached across the table and took one of her hands in his.

"We both screwed up," she assured him. "I assumed, with no evidence, that you were a rich-kid snob, but it turns out our backgrounds are quite similar."

She suddenly thought about that little rhyme Lois had recited earlier, and a smile tugged at her lips. "Or as Lois put it, you and I were both staying home from the circus to avoid being hurt."

He laughed.

Each of them lapsed into silence, just getting lost in the eyes of the other, and this time silence was awkward for neither of them.

The May nights still had a snap to them, and he had built a wood fire in the old nickle-and-brass stove. Not only had wood been chopped into neat stove lengths and piled nearby, but Hazel even made sure there was crumbled tree bark in a coffee can, for use as kindling. By now the flames reflected in the new polish of the floor and furniture, making them glow like embers.

He rose and moved around behind her chair, leaning down to embrace her and lightly kiss her hair.

He lowered his lips to kiss her neck, and she trembled with pleasure.

"Failure isn't always so bad, is it?" she asked him gently. "Hazel told me once that failure actually makes us more lovable because it makes us more human. You need to get over your perfectionist hang-up. I would still...love you even if you failed now and then."

"You know," he murmured low in her ear, his breath warm and tickly and exciting, "I actually believe that. After all, I failed to get that door open, didn't I? Yet you just said you love me."

"Hmm, that door. Did you really give it your best shot, Doctor, no pun?"

"Hell no," he confessed brazenly. "I'm not crazy. Hazel ad a good plan, and I wasn't about to blow it. Mad at ie?"

"Outraged," she fibbed, pretending to pout. "Now ou'll have to take your punishment like a man."

She turned her head just enough to put her lips in contact ith his.

Both of them found sudden release for their pent-up pas- on in a long, deep kiss.

"Tonight I'm a glutton for punishment," he told her, his reathing, like hers, heavier and less even now. "Can we o into the bedroom so you can *really* teach me a lesson?"

She searched his face. "I hate to point out the obvious, octor, but at the rate we're going, your real lesson may ome in about nine months."

He brought his face closer to hers. A secret smile tugged n his lips. "I love you, Becky, with all my heart I love ou. You're the one for me. I knew it practically the mo- ient I met you. If we produce a child from our union it ould be the second happiest day of my life."

"What would be the first?"

He stared at her deeply, his face taut with emotion. "Our edding day. Would you do me the great honor?"

Tears filmed her eyes, and emotion closed her throat gainst speech. She managed a nod.

He kissed her, his tongue, his lips dipping into her very oul. Slipping one arm under her legs, the other behind her ack, he easily lifted her. Once in the adjoining bedroom, e lowered her to the coverlet.

Two half-filled champagne glasses stood on the bedside ble from earlier. Candles provided a gentle, burnished ght.

He stood over the bed and raised his glass. "A toast," e said softly. "To Doctor and Mrs. John Saville and the ng, happy life they're going to share."

She sipped from his proffered glass. Already she wa
lightheaded from sheer joy and the heady course the nigl
had taken. The cold, arrogant snob she had invented in h
mind was dead and buried forever, along with the pa
Brian's treachery had caused her.

"Come here," he whispered, staring down at her.

She did.

He watched her, transfixed, while she rose to her knee
Slowly, languidly, she unfastened the white terry robe pro
vided by their ever-thoughtful hostess. The robe's edges fe
away, revealing white pearly skin bathed in the candleligh

When he started to remove his trousers and shirt he'
just thrown on, she playfully pulled him onto the bed wi
her.

"Allow me," she whispered. Running her hand dow
his unbuttoned shirt, she kissed his tautly muscled ches
reveling in the warm hard rock beneath her tongue.

Her lips moved lower, kissing his hard, flat stomach. H
hands slid between them, and he cupped her breasts to tea
the nipples erect with his fingers.

Impatient, he pulled her fully on top of him. He eas
first one, then the other nipple into his mouth. The delicio
heat made her gasp.

He slid off his shirt. She straddled him, holding tig
while he slid off his trousers. The white robe was nex
puddling uselessly on the floor.

His hands wound into the mass of her unbound hair. H
kissed her fiercely, then whispered, "I love you, Rebecc
I've needed you my whole life. At last, you're here," I
said as he slid every inch he had into her.

She gasped. Pleasure filled her. The want for more an
more of him drove her as she moved her hips with increa
ing speed and force.

His kiss satiated the hungry hollow of her mouth. I
moved harder and deeper inside her until she shudder

from the intense waves that gathered to the exploding point. In her mind, in her heart, all she saw, tasted and felt was him. All sense of time and place disappeared, taken over by the mindless ecstasy of newfound love.

He groaned his passion, coming deep inside her, and like a domino effect, he sent her crashing into her own release. She collapsed on top of him, exhausted by pleasure, enveloped by love.

Just before she drifted off, floating on a warm sea of bliss, he whispered in her ear, "May I assume you won't be looking for that new job after all?"

"You may," she whispered back. "But we just might have to discuss a generous maternity-leave policy, Doctor."

When Hazel finally unlocked the door on Friday morning, she was prepared to defend herself.

The first pleasant surprise was finding her two guests lingering over omelettes and coffee, looking very tired but very happy.

"Now don't get your innards in an uproar, you two," he greeted them. "I know what you're going to say, and —what?"

She stopped, surprised, when both of them burst out laughing.

"How's your heart this morning?" John teased her. "Any flutters? Or did we decide you had twitches?"

All three of them laughed.

Rebecca poured Hazel a mug of coffee, and she joined them at the table.

"Hazel," she told her friend fondly, giving her a quick hug. "You're too wicked to be pitied, you know that? And I love you for it."

This was a far better reception than Hazel had envisioned; indeed, she had even begun to regret her bold plan and feared their anger.

It was clear, however, after several failed schemes, that she had finally played the right trick. Not only was she vindicated as a master matchmaker, but her beloved town would have one more wonderful family to keep it alive and thriving.

"Happy now?" John demanded, grinning at her.

"Do-si-do and don't let go," she replied, singing it like a square-dance caller and evoking more laughter. "Well it's about time you two opened your damned eyes," she added in a lecturing tone, though from a joyful face. "It was as obvious as clown's makeup, to me and Lois, that you two belong together."

She squinted, spotting something on Rebecca's ring finger when the latter raised her cup to drink.

"What's that, honey?"

She and John exchanged a glance, and both laughed again. It was a ring fashioned from a horseshoe nail John had found in a cabinet.

"Hazel," he asked, "any chance you'd be interested in holding a wedding reception for us here at the ranch? As soon as next week, I mean?"

"Would I—well, is Paris a city? Of course I will! But my lands, why so soon, what's the hurry?"

"Because we're pretty sure," he replied, "that we've got less than nine months to tie the knot."

"And doctors," Rebecca added with a wink to him, "are seldom wrong about these things.

Epilogue

ois rolled her eyes at Hazel. "He's a nervous wreck. If
at baby doesn't come soon, they'll have to put him in the
spital."

Hazel stood at the patient sign-in almost rubbing her
nds in glee. "That's always the way. Doctors can handle
st about any complaint except their own."

"Tell me about it!" Rebecca chimed in from behind
ois, a stack of files in her hands.

"What are you doing carrying files? Let me take those!"
ois chided. "Do you want to give him a heart attack? It's
d enough you're still at work!"

Becky rubbed her blossomed middle with the absent-
inded contentedness of a mother-to-be. They'd been mar-
ed almost nine months but with John at her side, the time
emed to have flown. Perhaps because she was living the
e she'd always wanted, with her soul mate by her side,
d there weren't enough years to savor it all.

A soft smile touched her lips. She winked at Hazel. ''I Saville's been impossible. At night when we go home studies every move I make like I was some kind of n amoeba he'd just discovered in his microscope. Certain I'm not wishing anything upon you, Hazel, but one of tho ''flutters'' that put us in this state might be pretty welcon right now. The good doctor needs a mysterious illness get his attention off of—''

''Dr. Saville! Just the man I wanted to see!'' Hazel pip up, her face beaming at the frowning man who had j entered the reception area from his office.

''Great to see you, Hazel. How are you feeling?'' Jo asked, crooking his arm around his very pregnant wife.

''Fit as a fiddle,'' Hazel answered. ''This check-up's f you. I hear fatherhood's been wearing you out and y haven't even got to your first trail ride yet.''

He released a sexy, tired grin. ''Wearing me out? Th devil of a woman won't even let me come with her to t OB. Says I'm too obsessive.''

Rebecca laughed. ''You got that right, doctor. Save it f your own patients.''

''But his patients are so darned healthy!'' Lois added the ribbing.

John nodded, exasperated. ''She won't even tell me wh we're having. The decorator came to do the nursery, a Becky wouldn't let me know if she ordered pink or blue

Rebecca gave Hazel an aside gesture. In a mock whisp she said, ''He couldn't handle it.''

John stood behind the two, his arms crossed over h chest. ''I'm a physician. I've seen everything. I graduat top of my class at the best medical school this side of—

Hazel nodded to Rebecca in compliance. ''That's rig Becky. Better use the kid gloves with him. He's new this particular game, you know. Go gentle with him.''

Rebecca felt John's arms go around her. They we

strong and sure, and she knew, despite the teasing, they would see her through the next few days.

"All I'm asking for is the color of our baby's nursery. I don't think that's out of line given the fact that I was very much involved in the process of making this as-yet-un-color-coded baby," he grumbled.

Rebecca grinned. Her hand held his across her stomach as she smoothed over a kick. "Alright. I'll tell you." She winked again at Hazel. "Get out the smelling salts, gals, because he's got to know sooner or later, so I'm telling him now."

"And the color is—?" he prompted, nuzzling her.

"Pink *and* blue."

John stopped. He stared down at his wife in astonishment, his expression radiating his total love.

"See?" Rebecca shrugged at Hazel.

Hazel laughed. It was good to know her beloved town of Mystery would grow and flourish. It was even better knowing she had had a hand in the process.

"Where are you going, Hazel? After all," Rebecca cried out, laughing at her husband's overly protective embrace, "this is your fault too, you know."

"I take the blame gladly," Hazel quipped, with a secret smile of her own.

And she'd do it again, too.

The first chance she got.

* * * * *

January 2001
TALL, DARK & WESTERN
#1339 by Anne Marie Winston

February 2001
THE WAY TO A RANCHER'S HEART
#1345 by Peggy Moreland

March 2001
MILLIONAIRE HUSBAND
#1352 by Leanne Banks
Million-Dollar Men

April 2001
GABRIEL'S GIFT
#1357 by Cait London
Freedom Valley

May 2001
THE TEMPTATION OF
RORY MONAHAN
#1363 by Elizabeth Bevarly

June 2001
A LADY FOR LINCOLN CADE
#1369 by BJ James
Men of Belle Terre

MAN OF THE MONTH

For twenty years Silhouette has been giving
you the ultimate in romantic reads. Come join
the celebration as some of your favorite authors
help celebrate our anniversary with the most
sensual, emotional love stories ever!

Available at your favorite retail outlet.

Silhouette®
Where love comes alive™